[*The* THIRD EYE]

DAVID KNOWLES

NAN A. TALESE
DOUBLEDAY

New York • London • Toronto • Sydney • Auckland

[*The* THIRD EYE]

PUBLISHED BY NAN A. TALESE
an imprint of Doubleday
a division of Random House, Inc.
1540 Broadway, New York, New York 10036

DOUBLEDAY *is a trademark of Doubleday, a division of Random House, Inc.*

Book design by Fritz Metsch

Library of Congress Cataloging-in-Publication Data
Knowles, David, 1966–
The third eye / David Knowles. — 1st ed.
p.   cm.
I. Title.
PS3561.N677T48   2000
813'.54—dc21   99-33390
CIP

ISBN 0-385-49706-7
Copyright © 2000 by David Knowles
All Rights Reserved
Printed in the United States of America
March 2000
First Edition
1   3   5   7   9   10   8   6   4   2

To Jennifer,
whose name
is love

[*The* THIRD EYE]

Countless times in my life on this apartment-starved island, I have observed the Tuesday night queue as it forms in front of the Astor Place newsstand. Young people for the most part, nervously shifting their weight from side to side while they wait for the chance to scour the *Village Voice* newspaper classifieds. Intermittent tremors from passing subway trains tickle the bottoms of their tired feet. Curious pedestrians and taxi drivers slow down to see what they might be missing. Those on line are a desperate lot, too poor or full of pride to pay a Realtor to do the work for them, and astute enough to have figured out which kiosk first receives the weekly rental listings.

I think it's safe to say that Manhattan is the single toughest place to find affordable housing in the world, with Tokyo, or perhaps Paris, as a close second. In those crucial minutes when delivery trucks fan out across the city, these go-getters are already at work with their red pens, crossing out and circling prospective apartments. Not willing to waste the time it takes to walk home, they head straight for the nearest pay phone and encamp themselves. No precaution is too great in their search.

Like so many others on the rainy night of June 23, 1993, Maya Vanasi answered my own ad in the *Voice* the very same evening it ran. To most readers, the words must have seemed like an apparition. It was easily the best deal of the section.

Prime location, SoHo Sublet.
July 1 to Sept. 1. Pristine 1 BR
Hrdwd flrs. Air-con, $400/mo.
Call Jefferson @ (212) 496-3715

The phone rang continuously, from six o'clock until half past one in the morning. I sat at the kitchen table with my notepad, an assortment of just-delivered sushi, and a bottle of Riesling, listening to Chopin's waltzes at a volume loud enough for many of the callers to ask if someone was in fact playing the piano. Upon identifying the voice on the other end of the line as female, I gave out the address and a time for an interview. To the men I replied, "Regrettably, the apartment has been rented."

As I pen these words, I am trying to recall if there was anything in Maya's voice that told me she would be the lucky winner, but to say so would be a lie. I do remember having to ask her to repeat the spelling of both her first and last names, and, too, that she spoke with the slightest lilt of an Indian/ British accent. No, by the time I spoke to Maya I had already placed my bet on another woman, who sounded as if I'd granted her an unimaginable kindness in even scheduling an interview.

Wednesday morning I didn't bother with the phone, for the casual apartment hunter is not worth my time, but left the message machine on just in case. By ten-thirty the tape was filled with callers who must have known that they were far too late. I had two hours before the day's appointments would start arriving, so I went out and took breakfast at a nearby café. Continental fare: croissants, a cappuccino, two glasses of freshly squeezed orange juice, and a large bottle of Evian. Fluids are essential on days that I interview, as I have to talk so much.

Back at the apartment I set out all the items I needed on

the kitchen table. Yellow legal notepad with the list of names and times of each appointee, a stack of twenty-five blank applications, Polaroid camera, three new packages of film, and a bowl filled high with foil-wrapped chocolates.

12:15. I gave a last look around and was once again pleased to see what a fine job the cleaning service had done. Most applicants arrive early, so I wasn't surprised to hear the bell ring fifteen minutes in advance of the first appointment. I checked the list. "You must be Eva," I said into the intercom.

"I hope I'm not too early," she replied.

"Actually, could you give me just five minutes. I'm still tidying up."

"Sure . . . Five minutes?"

"Have a walk around the block and I'll be all set."

"Okay. Sorry."

"No problem at all." I darted over to the window and peered down at the street, making sure she wouldn't spot me. She stood looking up at the building, shielding her eyes from the sun with a large manila envelope. A stack of references, I guessed. She couldn't see me through the glare, and checked her watch before ambling along southward. Even from the fifth-story window I could tell she must be very pretty. Shoulder-length dark hair, trim figure, wearing a short black spaghetti-strap dress of the kind that was so popular that summer.

Exactly five minutes later, the bell sounded again and this time I buzzed her in, saying, "Fifth floor, the door's to the right at the end of the hallway." I unlocked the dead bolt and stood in the open sliver of the doorway listening to her footsteps as she climbed the stairs. They were quick and energetic for the first three flights, then slowed on the last two—a normal pattern. I attribute it not only to the strain of climbing the five-story walkup, but also to the desire of the applicant to appear composed when she meets me. And composed Eva was as she rounded the banister into view, with a freshly applied coat of shiny scarlet lipstick and her hair combed just so. Not just pretty, I thought. Model pretty. I opened the door wider and stepped across the threshold into the hall.

"Jefferson?" she asked. I replied with a nod. "I'm Eva Wilson." She walked toward me, her hand outstretched.

"How do you do, Eva." I took her soft, thin hand and gave it just the slightest squeeze. Right away I pegged her for an aspiring actress, and I do stress aspiring. She fluttered her eyelashes and even concocted a knowing glance as if to suggest an attraction between us. After thirty years on this planet, I have learned enough to know that a young woman of her physical caliber is not swayed by the likes of mine upon first glance. Bluntly put, I'm not a handsome man. Ever since puberty I've known as much. It's the shape of my face. My father's large forehead, my mother's tiny nose and ears. The combination just doesn't come together in an aesthetically pleasing way. Throughout my painful adolescence, whenever I entered a classroom, girls would burst into giggling fits. By the time I entered college, their mockery had faded into something even more vicious, silent indifference.

I haven't fared much better as an adult. Beautiful women never let their eyes rest upon my face for too long. A momentary assessing glance, and they continue on their way. Don't think me self-pitying, I simply know my odds and am not easily seduced by actors, but that doesn't mean I didn't enjoy Eva's little performance.

I had to laugh at the way she caught her breath when she got her first look at the foyer and living room beyond. Her gasp! I still hear it, the kind scripted into Broadway musicals. In the far reaches of the balconies of the St. James or Miller Theater they'd have heard this gasp. You see, some less scrupulous landlords might have advertised my apartment as a two-bedroom, counting the eight-by-eleven entrance hall as a legitimate space for sleeping. But what kind of living is that? To open one's door directly onto unmade sheets?

"I love it," she said, though she hadn't yet seen the bedroom, bath, or kitchen. "I love it. I'll take it."

"Slow down. First let me give you the complete tour and then we'll talk."

"I'm just saying I know I want it. I already know. You wouldn't believe the dumps I've been in today. This place is beautiful. I love it. The rugs, the wood floors, the details." No, she wasn't acting these lines, and it caused me a pang of sympathy for what these young people go through.

"Thank you very much."

We walked into the living room, her smile contagious. She flitted about the place, from the windows, to the fireplace, the bookshelves, and back around again. Next I showed her to the bedroom.

"The windows are so beautiful. What kind of wood is this?" I suppose she wanted to sound discerning.

"Oak. The original, from 1885."

"It's in such good condition. Really incredible. I love how you've kept them uncovered. Does the place get direct sun?"

"Not direct unfortunately. But in the early morning the light reflects off the abandoned building across the street, and that's enough for the plants to live on." I pointed out the large dracaena and mother-in-law's tongue. "They'll be your only real duty. I'm very fond of them, so you'll have to promise to take good care of them."

"I love plants. How much water do they take?" She went to the window and considered the boarded-up face of the building that I had referred to.

"I'll leave you instructions. The kitchen's next if you're ready."

"I'm ready."

By this time delirium had taken hold of her, and she strolled through the foyer like a first-time tourist of Venice or Prague. She had heard that apartments of this caliber existed in Manhattan, but until then had never been inside one, much less had the opportunity to inhabit one. In her eyes I could see her repressed middle-class dreams emerging as if from a long hibernation. Not since her parents' house in Connecticut or Vermont or wherever had she been able to live in such comfort, but here, if only for two short months, she would reclaim her rightful place as a member of a higher caste.

"Have a seat." I pulled the chair for her and she made a hum intoning her delight.

"Such a gentleman."

"There are, of course, a few questions that I ask all the applicants."

"Of course."

I took my own chair across the table from her. "Please, help yourself to a chocolate," I said.

"No thanks."

Why is it, I often wonder, that we Americans are taught that it's more polite to refuse than accept a simple gesture of hospitality? No, I wasn't going to let her get out of it so easily. "Really, I insist. They're absolutely delicious." I held the bowl out for her, so she really didn't have a choice.

"Okay. Thank you." She took one, but hesitated before unwrapping it.

"Go on, enjoy it!"

Seeing no way out, she removed the cherry liqueur–filled ball of chocolate from the foil and plopped the whole thing in her mouth. This I silently applauded, as some past applicants have chosen to bite it in half and cradle the uneaten portion in their palms like the broken shell of an egg dripping yolk and white. Placing the whole chocolate in one's mouth is no small feat either, and I relished the expression on her face in the minute or so I gave her to chew before I asked my first question.

As it turned out, Eva did not get the apartment. A pity that someone so utterly qualified in other categories—looks, enthusiasm—should be disqualified for such a minor infraction. Her disqualifying mark? A German shepherd she was not willing to part with. Some rules I cannot bend. Dogs, especially big, loud, attack-style dogs who tear up furniture and scratch wood floors, do not fit with my scenario, period, no exceptions.

The look on her face when I told her not to bother with the application! Winded, crushed, defeated. Knowing she'd never do as well as this place, perhaps she thought about giving up her dream of moving to New York right then and there. She pictured herself heading off back to the suburbs, settling for her old room at Mother and Dad's—the shelves filled with stuffed animals and soccer trophies. On the other hand, if you can't get rid of a dog to live in the apartment of your dreams, then maybe you don't have what it takes to live in this city.

"There's no way?" she pleaded. "I mean, he's a well-behaved dog. He doesn't bark—"

"I'm sorry. It's really a shame."

"So that's it?" She looked at the floor and gently ground the soul of her left pump into the terra-cotta tile. "There's really no way . . ." She was searching for alternatives that didn't exist.

The interview had run its course, but I couldn't quite accept the fact that I'd probably never see her again. I picked up the Polaroid camera. "Let me take your picture so I'll remember your face. If you change your mind or find the dog a new home, you can give me a call."

"You want to take my picture?"

"Terrible with names, and I have to interview over twenty people today. Never forget a face though."

Her spirits sank further still at the realization that her chances had all but evaporated. I lifted the camera to my eye and she did her best to reconstruct an approximation of her smile. "One . . . two . . . three." Out popped the day's first portrait. Just then the buzzer rang. "You see?" I told her. "Here come the hordes."

She picked up her purse and papers and tried to think of something else to say but was too discouraged. I followed her to the door. Yes, it was indeed a pity all around.

"Thank you anyway," she managed as she shook my hand. Then, miraculously, her spirits lifted. It was as if she'd been staring at an impenetrable Scrabble board and suddenly found a way to construct a one-hundred-point word. She nearly squeezed the blood out of my hand. "Actually, you know what?"

I raised an eyebrow. "No, what?"

"I just remembered that my uncle said he'd take care of the dog if I needed him to."

"Your uncle?"

"He lives in New Jersey."

"Really?"

"I mean it's only for two months, right? I guess I wasn't thinking in those terms, but there's no reason why I couldn't just leave the dog with him and pick him up at the end of the summer. It's not far if I wanted to visit."

I did my best to play along, but I realized that regardless of her promises, if I let her have the place, she'd be sure to try and smuggle in the pooch. "Why don't you call him tonight and let me know what he says."

"Oh, he already said he would. It's not a problem. Really it's not."

The buzzer sounded again, this time for an unpleasantly long duration. "Call me tonight," I said with no intention of talking to her again. "At seven."

"At seven. I'll call at seven," she repeated in a breathy voice that clung to the tattered remnants of an opportunity gone awry. She brandished a flirtatious smile in a last-ditch attempt and only reluctantly let go of my hand before turning away.

The buzzer yelled out for a third, ugly time just as I shut the door behind her. Before I answered the intercom, I retrieved my yellow pad and Eva's nearly developed Polaroid from the table. Yes, the picture at least was turning out to be a terrific success. "Susan?" I called into the intercom.

"No," a loud and shrill voice replied, "Kendra."

"Kendra? Your appointment isn't for twenty minutes yet."

"What time is it? My watch says I'm only ten minutes early."

"I'll tell you what, wait five minutes, and if the next girl hasn't arrived, you can come up."

I heard her laughing through her nose. "Girl?" she said under her breath, not realizing the sensitivity of the intercom microphone. "Can't I just see the place now?"

"I'm sorry." Already I had heard enough to know that Kendra's chances were slim at best.

How plain they all seem in retrospect when compared with Maya. As I shuffle through their Polaroids, I'm hard pressed to find another who even approaches her grace, or what I think I recollect as her grace. Yet when I replay our interview in my mind, I realize that what attracted me to her was not merely her looks or the sharpness of her wit, but something altogether intangible. Unlike the other tenants, whose lives were so easy to read, I had no preconceptions as to how her stay might turn out. If I were to ask a therapist's opinion—and in weaker moments I've considered doing so—he or she might cite the fact that I found myself craving a less predictable relationship with my tenant. That my actions belied an unconscious desire to change my modus operandi. Of course I won't pretend I understand the nature of how the human mind works—my own included—but for the record, I never outwardly felt like I wanted to change anything.

At three o'clock, disheartened that I was still without a single suitable candidate for the apartment, I took a lunch break. Beef carpaccio, a plate of pasta, Barbaresco wine, and an arugula salad sounded like just the things to reinvigorate me, so I headed to a tried-and-true spot two blocks away. You could say I'm something of a food fetishist. When they hit, my cravings are specific down to the last course. Just another reason to live in New York, where you're always assured of finding what you want no matter the time of day or type of cuisine.

Perhaps my passion for eating comes from the fact that neither one of my parents can cook. Growing up, we ate out nearly every night of the week, which I hated as a child. I yearned for normalcy. Meat loaf night, and leftovers. But when it came time to shop, wade through recipe books, battle the stove, and do the dishes, I grew more sympathetic to my parents' lifestyle.

The restaurant was nearly empty. I sat out on the open patio, the sun and clouds taking turns with the light on my page as I flipped through *Art View* magazine. Just before the carpaccio arrived, a full-page ad caught my eye—an announcement for a Charles Hardigan show at Rent Space gallery on West Broadway. Hardigan is a minimalist sculptor whom I took an interest in some years ago. I make my living using foresight, both in real estate and art, and I was fortunate enough to purchase a half dozen of his works five months before he died. At the time, I remember wondering if they weren't overpriced. The week following his death, I sold them for five times the amount.

Hardigan's pieces, most of them installations, are about— if one can be so bold as to define abstract art in such concrete terms—transforming the psychological boundaries of space, about balance and psychic tension. He might, for example, place a single golden rod in the center of the floor of a long, empty room, and in doing so utterly change the mood of the place. My particular fondness for his work dates back several years, to his first major solo show at the prestigious Costanzo Gallery.

The installation featured differing types of metal rods— copper, brass, steel, aluminum, lead, and bronze—in relation to the otherwise stark white rooms. I attended on a packed Saturday afternoon, because audience response is one of my favorite parts of contemporary art. Though I spend more than enough money at Costanzo to receive private tours of the exhibitions, I always refuse in favor of the normal business hours crowd. I thrive on their confusion, their displays of disgust—hissing, rolled eyes, hands thrown in the air—the kind art on the leading edge incites. Not surprisingly, the abstract nature of Hardigan's installation baffled more than a few of the gallery goers.

In the second room, entitled "Square Iron Rod on Floor," two young Japanese women whispered back and forth to one another before bursting out into little fits of laughter. These grown women covered their mouths with their hands like schoolkids, a gesture that only made their scorn stand out more. Such white faces! Powdered over and painted with black mascara and dark burgundy lipstick. They moved on to the far corner of the room and the third piece, entitled "Octagonal Copper Rod Standing in Corner." I decided to follow, finding their tittering a compelling reaction to the ambiguous mood of the art.

Each wore varying shades of black from head to toe—one in a short skirt, sheer tights, and go-go boots, the other in pleated pants and laced, sensible shoes, both with button-up blouses and matching turtlenecks underneath. Their lipstick, red nail polish, and the gold Gucci insignia on a black patent-leather purse provided the only swipes of color on either one of them. I maintained an unobtrusive distance as they continued their childlike whispering. Then, out of nowhere, it happened. In a synchronized display, the light in the room glimmered off the purse's Gucci emblem and the polished copper rod. In that subtle and beautiful instant the women ceased to exist as spectators. They fused so completely with the artwork that I felt compelled to rewrite the titles of the pieces as I went. "Two Japanese Women Whispering Next to Octagonal Copper Rod

Standing in Corner" and "Women in Black Laughing at Aluminum Pole Hung from Ceiling with Wire."

With hardly a glance at the lead pipe affixed to the ceiling
of the last room, the women started down the exit stairs. I stood
there dumbfounded, overcome by a tremendous sense of loss. It
was as if the subject matter had broken free from its proper
frame of reference. Like a ballerina in a Degas suddenly standing and walking off the canvas.

Downstairs, the women loitered a short while on the steps
before stepping out into the sea of people that strolled along
Broadway. It was a cool, windy day, with the kind of light that
told you winter wasn't far away. Arm in arm, they started to
cross Prince Street. Just then a Rastafarian bicycle messenger
swerved in front of them. I watched from the corner as his arm
grazed the woman's Gucci purse as he sped by. The black handbag swung up over her shoulder, and her tiny body convulsed
with fear. Her friend clutched her by the arm and pulled her to
the other side of the street, where they covered their mouths
with disbelief and shot angry looks after the messenger. To my
eyes it was all a beautifully executed drama of spatial dynamics,
and I give full credit to Charles Hardigan for putting me in the
right frame of mind to appreciate the larger whole.

I've come to think of this episode as a watershed in my life.
It was the first time I acknowledged that I'd started to register
the everyday world first and foremost in terms of aesthetics. A
silently metastasizing cancer, this way of seeing things probably
began as far back as high school. Eventually, I found myself
powerless to distinguish between art and real life. In supermarket aisles I often lose myself in a critique of colorful label patterns and packaging construction. The symmetry of rows of
soup cans, bottles of beer. The haphazard jumble of the cheese
display case, as though painstakingly crafted for my contempla-

tion. At intersections I marvel at the splintering geometry of traffic patterns. The beautiful drama of stoplights, speeding heaps of metal, and the gold and white lines that try to govern them is always enough to entertain me for half an hour or so. Far and away, however, human interaction, with its myriad variations, holds the greatest thrill. People are truly the best subject matter going.

I've become a curator of the aesthetics of everyday life, but I'd never be so presumptuous as to claim this way of looking at the world is in any way unique. Many before me have employed the same method of viewing reality. "Devouring images," as William Burroughs put it. It's merely an exaggeration of natural impulses that we all share. Every waking moment we judge the beauty or ugliness of those around us. Our brains relentlessly evaluate, choose, and order experience on an aesthetic basis. I have simply chosen to raise the volume at which those evaluating voices speak, to extract the artistic content from the everyday whenever possible. Photographers and filmmakers are especially prone to this behavior. Think of the old cliché image of a director raising his hands to imitate a frame as he catches sight of something he fancies. Perhaps that's the best way to describe it, an insistent need to frame.

●

I had left myself an hour between appointments and got back from lunch with five minutes to spare. To my surprise, the stoop of my building was empty as I approached. Whoever the next contestant might be, she was not as eager as the others before her.

Upstairs I took up my list again and practiced her last name aloud, altering between two possible pronunciations. "Vanasi," then "Vanasi." The grandfather clock in the hall chimed four, and the intercom buzzer spoke a short and courteous reply.

I pushed the talk button. "Maya?"

"Yes. Mr. Jefferson?"

"Just Jefferson, not mister."

"Sorry?"

"Come on up. Fifth floor, door's on the right."

"Thank you."

Her accent was much more evident than it had been the night before. Mr. Jefferson, I said to myself with a shake of the head. In part my amusement stemmed from the fact that unknowingly she'd gotten it right. I donned the name Jefferson to help conceal my identity and add a bit of flair to the experiment. Though I used it as my given name, it was actually inspired by the president of the same surname. An intensely private man who rose to the nation's most public office, the real Jefferson's murky legacy had always fascinated me. That author of the great doctrine on individual rights, who also held slaves. To be sure, his proclivity toward architecture also played a part in choosing the name.

I unlocked the dead bolt and drew up a mental picture of a plump, middle-aged Indian woman wrapped in a purple and green sari. Strangely, as I waited in the doorway I heard no sounds of approaching footsteps. After ten or fifteen seconds of sustained silence I returned to the intercom and pushed the door button again, suspecting that she hadn't made it in on the first try. For good measure I called into the two-way speaker. "Did you get in all right?"

No answer. I went back to the door and was startled to find a serene-looking young woman standing in the hall as if she'd been waiting there for some time. Her presence caught me off guard and I must have jumped back a bit.

"Excuse me," she apologized. "Did I frighten you?"

"No, no, I'm fine. Hello. Are you . . ."

"Maya Vanasi. I'm sorry if I frightened you."

This was Maya Vanasi? My mental concoction bore no resemblance to the beauty before me. She was on the tall side, five foot eight, my guess. Maybe an inch shorter than me. Jet-black hair that fell straight down her back without the slightest hint of a curl. Smooth dark skin that might have placed her in any number of ethnic groups. A lithe build, but nothing boyish about its curving Shape. She wore western clothing. Jeans and a loose-fitting short-sleeve navy blouse. Black leather sandals, assorted silver bracelets, small hoop earrings, and a stud in the left nostril.

One adornment above all the others, however, caught my interest—a circular red mark, perhaps a quarter of an inch in

diameter, painted just between her eyebrows. I had always associated the dot with Hinduism but knew little else about it. For
the moment that we stood in the doorway, I found I could not
take my eyes from it. In fact, the more I tried to look away, the
more futile it became to do anything but stare directly into the
little red void. Normally, I'm not impressed by material displays
of religious symbolism, but the dot seemed to put her face into
perfect balance.

Fortunately, Maya did not seem to mind my fascination.
"Tilaka," she said.

"Tikala?"

"Ti-la-ka. Some call it the third eye, the window to the
soul."

"To whose soul? Yours?"

She smiled. Perhaps I asked the question a tad too ear-
nestly. I had no idea whether she was making fun of me or not.
Frankly, just watching her gave me so much pleasure that I
didn't care if the joke had come at my expense. I felt an almost
boyhood awe at her beauty, and yet as strange as it sounds, I
cannot remember the specifics of her face. I do know that the
word *resplendent* kept going through my mind. In the past, I'd
only ever experienced this kind of memory deficit with artwork.
Frequently, I've gone to museums, stood in front of famous
works for a good length of time, returned home, and found I
couldn't reconstruct one of the picture's details even though the
overall sensory impression remained clear.

"May I come in?" she asked.

"Please do. Where are my manners?" I stood clear of the
door and gave a shallow bow as she passed. "I'll give you the
grand tour."

She stepped in and looked at the kitchen. I remember
noting that her clothes looked brand new—jeans not yet faded,

her shirt pressed with crisp edges. The bracelets shined like they'd just been polished. "You sounded as though you'd be many years older from the way you spoke on the telephone," she said as she opened the refrigerator and gave a peek at the shelves holding a few stray condiments and the leftover California rolls.

"You're not the first to say so. The fridge will be completely cleared out by the time I leave."

"What room is next?"

We continued on, and she kept such a straight face that I had no idea whether or not she even liked the place. In the bedroom I mentioned the bit about the plants and she turned and touched the soil. "This dracaena is in need of water."

Never had I witnessed such indifference toward the apartment or such calm in an applicant. She regarded the possessions around her like she might be their rightful owner and had come to reclaim what was already hers. All, that is, except for my worthy reproduction of Degas's famous painting "Interior." I commissioned the piece three summers ago from my good friend and partner, Henry. At that time he was a painter of considerable promise, and I did my best to help foster his career. His rendering of "Interior" hangs above the fireplace, and our tour halted there while she stood fully absorbed by it. Many applicants don't even notice the piece in their haste, so Maya's reaction pleased me.

The painting is based on the climactic scene from Emile Zola's novel *Thérèse Raquin*. A woman and a man occupy opposite corners of a bedroom. She sits hunched over on a footstool, facing away from him. Her shadowed profile reveals an expression of scorn, or sorrow, or extreme disappointment. The gentleman, meanwhile, is backed up against the door. He gazes across the room in the direction of a glowing fire and seems to share in her despair and helplessness. His hands in his pants pockets, he has drifted away in thought. But why try to re-create Zola's scene when he can speak for me?

> Laurent carefully closed the door behind him and remained for a moment leaning against it looking into the room with a worried, embarrassed expression. A bright fire blazed on the hearth, throwing out patches of yellow that danced on the ceiling and the walls. The room was thus full of a lively, flickering light, in the midst of which the lamp on the table seemed pale. . . . Thérèse was sitting on a low chair to the right of the hearth, with her chin in her hand and her eyes fixed on the bright flames. She did not turn her head when Laurent entered.

And the cause for the painting's mournful tone? A plan gone awry. Two years prior, the lovers plotted and carried out the murder of the woman's impotent husband. After successfully disposing of the corpse, they put their affair on hold so as to avert the townspeople's suspicion. Jump ahead now to the scene of the painting. The couple's long-awaited wedding night. Strewn on the stretch of floor between the newlyweds, her discarded corset peeks out from the shadows. Tellingly, the bed covers remain undisturbed. We spy a married couple's failed attempt at resurrecting their dormant passion. The same impotence that precipitated the murder now resides with them.

Maya Vanási's eyes scrutinized the length and breadth of the canvas. She wasn't bothered by the silence of the room or the fact that I watched her as she stared at the painting. "Degas," I explained. "A copy, but a very good copy, don't you think?"

"I haven't seen the original, so there's no way I could know for sure."

"That's true. You'll have to take my word for it." For the first few seconds I was content to observe her fascination, finding it unlikely that the painting was actually moving her in such a dramatic fashion. The look in her eyes was a bit eerie. "Interior" captured her attention in a way that we of the cynical age might not believe possible. Nothing disingenuous about her pose, unlike the teenage girls at the Metropolitan Museum who mine the canvases for the inflated emotions of adolescence. No, if Degas, or Henry for that matter, were to see Maya's reaction, he might burst into tears of joy. I turned my own eyes up at the painting to find out what warranted such a prolonged study. For two or three minutes we gazed wordlessly at the fire's warm light upon the woman's bare shoulder and the gentleman's far-off, bitter expression as he leaned against the door.

What did Maya see? What caused her to stand so still and straight without a hint of emotion on her face? It sounds ludicrous as I reread these words; after all, "Interior" is one of my favorite pieces. Of all people, I, who commissioned the reproduction, should know what it is that could give this young woman pause. Perhaps over time I have exhausted the image, which isn't to say it doesn't still please me, just that at that moment I saw the same set of emotions and references I always had. Zola's story, the murder. The fire hissing and cracking. Embers crumbling into ash. Decay.

"May I see the bathroom?" she asked, breaking away from Degas as though she had merely been counting the number of electrical outlets in the room.

"Of course." We walked back through the bedroom and I opened the door for her.

With the most deliberate sense of purpose, she turned on

the tub faucet to check the pressure, then got down on her knees and measured the tub's width using the distance from her elbow to her fingertips as a ruler—an ancient Egyptian technique, if I'm not mistaken. It all looked very odd.

"I think you'll fit," I said.

"It's a quirk of mine. I'm partial to measurements. Like to know exactly what I'm in for."

"Me too."

She stood up and smiled. "It's decided then. I am interested in renting the flat."

"You're sure the bathtub meets your needs?" I chided one last time.

She smiled. "Quite sure."

"Okay, then. Well, why don't we have a seat? There are a few things that I like to ask my applicants, I'm sure you understand."

"I understand."

At the kitchen table I tried to organize my scattered thoughts. I had the greatest temptation to forgo the usual questions and simply hand over the keys to her. But why? Why had she charmed me so? Because she appreciated one of my favorite paintings? Or that she employed archaic measuring techniques, or adorned her forehead with a red dot? My rational side finally spoke up. The inquiry would not be swayed by emotion. If she turned out to be the one to rent the apartment, it would be because she met each of my stringent requirements. The criteria had been drawn with a specific purpose in mind, that purpose being my own safety. One small mistake might spell disaster.

"Have a chocolate," I suggested.

"No thank you."

"Really, I insist. They're absolutely delicious." Following

the steps of my well-practiced routine, I lifted the bowl, but as I looked at her face, my eyes floated up again to the red tilaka. I knew it was impolite to stare that way, but I couldn't help it.

She offered her delicate smile again. "I'm afraid I don't eat chocolate," she replied.

Rather than press the point as I had done all day long, I retracted the bowl and set it back down on the table. "Yes, of course, how rude of me. Is it on account of religious beliefs? Something about cows, is that it?"

She seemed perched on the verge of laughter. "No, I suffer from food allergies."

I had been duped by my own romanticism. "How awful. Just chocolate?"

"No, many things. Certain kinds of wheat and yeast."

"That's terrible. I can't imagine. Eating is such a pleasure. It must be awful to have to restrict your diet."

"Have you never had to give something up?"

"Absolutely, but not without plenty of grudges and regrets and tantrums."

She laughed through her nose, and for a fleeting moment I felt like I had connected with her. I picked up my yellow pad and flipped to the page filled with my list of questions. "All right, then, Miss Vanasi, a few words about the apartment. Can you keep a secret?"

"When I put my mind to it."

"Nothing earth-shattering, just that I'm subletting against the will of my landlord. It's safe to say that if he were to find out about this little arrangement, he'd be quite upset, possibly even threaten me with eviction. It's a delicate situation but one that has worked out quite well over the previous four summers. Therefore I must insist on a few points to insure my own peace of mind while I'm away."

"Where will you go?"

"Guatemala, to shoot the jaguars that live in the rain forest."

She seemed puzzled at my verbiage.

"Take photographs. It's what I do for a living. I'm a professional photographer. Wildlife primarily. Never been to Central America, so I decided to lengthen the stay into a full-fledged holiday. They say the Mayan ruins aren't without their charms."

She looked directly into my eyes, but gave away precious little of her thoughts.

"Now," I continued, "to start with. Do you plan to keep regular hours?"

"Regular hours?"

"You're not a night-crawler, a late-night kind of person, arriving home at three or four in the morning? It's the neighbors I'm worried about. Mrs. Adolfo downstairs in particular. Seventy-four and a bit sensitive to noise. She's sure to complain if you're up walking around on the hardwood past midnight or so."

"I won't be coming in late."

"Very good. The same logic applies to parties."

"I won't be having any parties."

"And if possible a minimum of gentleman callers."

Here she tilted her head ever so slightly, and I thought sure that I saw the beginnings of a smile lurking at the corners of her mouth.

"What I mean to say is do what you will but just make sure you do it quietly. Next, let's see. Pets. Do you have any pets?"

She shook her head.

"Excellent. And you seem like you'll be good with the plants. I know it's silly, but I do worry about them."

"People keep all manner of pets," she said.

"Yes, they do. Are you currently employed in the city?"

"No. I have just arrived from India."

"But you do have the means to pay the rent?"

"Yes. Money is not a worry."

"I'll need you to pay both months up front, and I have to insist on cash. Is that a problem?"

"I have no bank account here, so I'm glad you didn't ask for a check."

"What part of India do you come from?" I asked.

"Banaras. You are familiar with India?"

"Not well. Banaras you say?"

"That is the old name. Most foreigners know it that way. Now we call it Varanasi."

"Like your last name?"

"Similar, but my name is Vanasi."

"It's pretty. Does it mean anything?"

"How does the expression go? 'What's in a name?' "

"Ah, Shakespeare. *Romeo and Juliet,* right? 'Forsake thy father and refuse thy name . . . A rose by any other,' et cetera, et cetera."

"You must take a little time and learn about Banaras. A very important city in all of India and in the history of the world."

"You don't say?"

"Absolutely." She didn't elucidate, nor did I press her.

"May I ask why it is you decided to come to New York?"

"Yes you may ask, but some questions don't have an immediate answer."

"That's all right. New York's the kind of place you don't need a specific reason to visit. Do you have family here?"

"No family. They are all back in India, except for my father's cousin who owns a shop in Manchester, England."

"Really? Have you been to visit him?"

"Before I arrived in New York."

"What did you think?"

"The people there have a great spirit."

"They do?" This certainly didn't square with the picture the city had left me with. Such bleak industrialism. A deadly combination when mixed with that droll English sensibility of accepting one's lot in life. Never had I felt so American as when I sat in the pubs of Manchester and listened to one thoroughly depressing existence after another. "I'd have to disagree with you there."

Here was her smile again—a lime-green blade of grass sprouting between the cracks of a sidewalk deep in the middle of a New York winter, incongruous and so completely refreshing. The buzzer sounded, catching us both off guard. She took in a quick breath and widened her eyes with surprise, that look I come so close to remembering. For the first time that afternoon, I saw something resembling vulnerability, and it is that single image of her I return to so often in my thoughts, like a cracked, dilapidated photograph of a sweetheart kept in a soldier's wallet.

I checked my watch and was shocked our twenty minutes was up. We must have stood in front of "Interior" longer than I realized.

"Is it another person for the apartment?" she asked.

Shame rose up inside me. I felt as though I'd betrayed her. "Yes, but just between you and me, I think that your chances are quite good."

Was she disappointed that I hadn't guaranteed her the place, or happy that she was a prominent candidate? Her face was a Rorschach inkblot, and I was a blind man. The buzzer again.

She stood up. "I must go. You're very busy I can see."

"Please leave me a number where I can reach you."

"I'm sorry, but there's no line in the room of my hotel."

"No phone in the hotel room? Where on earth are you staying?"

"A place in Harlem."

"In Harlem? What in God's name are you doing staying in Harlem?"

"You don't like it there?"

"Listen, can you call me? Can you get to a phone tonight?"

"Yes. What time shall I call?"

"How about eight o'clock?" This was ludicrous. I knew that I had already chosen her, so why not just come out and say it?

"Yes, I will call at eight. Thank you, sir." She turned toward the door, and before I could open it for her, she slipped out into the hall and down the stairs with those light and soundless steps.

Shit, I thought. Forgot to take the Polaroid.

●

S uffice it to say that the following seven interviews did not measure up to Maya's. Though I did select two women as suitable backups, I can't say they excited me much. Yes, I can see from their pictures that both were very pretty, but my mind had seized upon one thing only. With each successive applicant my conviction grew stronger. Maya Vanasi from Banaras, India, would be this summer's tenant.

Seven forty-five. I plugged the phone back in and found it was ringing. "Hello?"

"Jefferson? It's me, Eva, from this morning. Eva Wilson, you remember, the one who had the dog? I've been trying to get through since seven, like you said, but there was no answer."

"Yes, hello, Eva. What can I do for you?"

"I talked to my uncle and it's all fine with him. He'll take the dog for July and August. So is it okay?"

"Eva, I certainly wish that it was, but I'm afraid that the very next applicant ended up taking the place. She already put down the deposit, in fact."

"But I thought you said that if I took care of the dog, the apartment was mine."

"I'm sorry if we've had a misunderstanding. The apartment is no longer avail—" She hung up before I could finish the sentence. You can't please everyone, I reassured myself, least of all actresses.

Seven-fifty, the phone rang again. A latecomer hoping for a tour of the apartment. Seven fifty-five, another frustrated applicant. Eight o'clock. It was a new and disconcerting sensation to be the one awaiting confirmation. Usually I made those phone calls. In fact, I admit that on a few occasions I even took pleasure drawing out the hours so as to heighten the sense of suspense.

I paced a circuitous route leading from the kitchen to the foyer to the living room, where I'd glance up at the Degas, then back through the foyer and past the kitchen phone. Two steps into the living room, on my third such loop, the phone rang out and I turned on my heel.

"Hello?"

"Mr. Jefferson?"

"Ms. Vanasi?"

"Yes, good evening."

"Good evening to you too." How wonderful to hear her smooth, lilting voice again. "I'm happy to report that the apartment is yours for the taking. Are you still interested?"

"Yes I am." Her tone was calm, but not the contrived calm someone like Eva would have no doubt portrayed. Then again, she didn't sound very excited that she had won the competition either. Perhaps she'd seen my place on her first day of looking, I thought, and hadn't recognized what an exceptional bargain she had found. How quickly I jumped to her defense!

"Okay then. I'm taking off for Guatemala City a week from Monday. But let's talk for a moment about the meantime. Are you quite sure you're all right up there in Harlem?"

"Yes, I'm sure. Why, what is the problem?"

"I don't want to get you worried. More than likely, there's

no problem at all. It's just that there are dangerous parts of this city, and you have to be careful. The hotel, is it on a good block? Are you comfortable there?"

"It is quite adequate."

"What's the name?" I wasn't sure why I had asked. I wasn't likely to recognize the name of anything above Seventy-second Street.

"The Old Memorial Hotel," she replied.

"What?" I yelled.

"What's wrong? Is something wrong?"

I had come across the very name not two days ago in a *Times* article. Dirty cops shaking down a drug dealer. A sting operation gone awry, the paper reported. Two dead, three wounded. "Listen carefully, Maya, that is not a safe place. I want you to check out at once and take a cab downtown. You can start staying here immediately."

"Dangerous? No, I don't think so. It is a very friendly place, and the rooms are large."

"This is serious, Maya, I assure you. The neighborhood is full of drugs and corrupt police. It's not safe. Believe me, I'm not the squeamish type, but that place simply will not do."

"But what about you? Where will you live?"

"I have another apartment not far away."

"Another apartment?" The line fell silent, and I wondered what expression she might be wearing. I don't know why, but my intuition told me she was smiling.

"Just around the corner, in fact. Where I have my photographic studio, store my equipment. There's a bed that's very comfortable. I sleep there all the time. You won't be putting me out in the slightest." What compelled me to offer up such truthful information? One after the other I continued breaking my own rules for this stranger. The curse of hindsight is that it allows you to identify a pattern in your own behavior. And here, with the apartment admission, I clearly committed an error of judgment.

"No," she replied. "I thank you for your generosity, but I'll be fine here until the first of the month."

"Don't be silly."

"Thank you, Mr. Jefferson, really, but my answer is no. Please tell me when I should meet you again so I can pay you the rent."

I wasn't going to win this argument and didn't want to come off as overbearing. "The first will be fine. My flight doesn't leave until the late afternoon. Is that day convenient?"

"What time shall I arrive?"

"Noon, we'll have lunch nearby. Meet me here at the apartment. Listen, if you won't accept my offer, then at the very least check into some other hotel farther downtown. I can recommend several."

"I'm paid up already, and it's quite fine I assure you. Please, don't worry. I'm very able to take care of myself."

Evidently there was nothing more to say.

"So I'll see you in ten days, Mr. Jefferson. Thank you very much."

"Okay, Maya. Congratulations."

She hung up. I bent down, unplugged the phone, and started my pacing all over again. Ten days. Ten days! An eternity. My mind raced with worries about what her stay at the Old Memorial might hold for her, but at the same time I was ecstatic that she had agreed to rent the apartment. I resolved to wake early the next morning and visit the public library. Maybe I'd find out something about Banaras and the significance of the mark on her forehead.

A night of restless half-sleep ensued. I tossed about in bed until three or four, never finding a comfortable position. My imagination concocted a terrible image and stuttered over it for hours on end until there was no choice but to regard it as a possible premonition. The image? A little stream of blood flowing from Maya Vanasi's third eye. It trickled down the bridge of her nose, then on to the tip, where a single crimson tear perched, quivered, and then fell away.

●

Friday morning the skies promised heavy rain. Thunder murmured in the direction of New Jersey. The air was thick with humidity, but my cabdriver hadn't opted for the air conditioner yet. As I stepped out onto the curb, occasional sun streams pierced through gaps in the towering clouds and flickered bright light on the white marble face of the public library. It looked as though a giant movie projector had been pointed down at the building, and I stood gazing up at the effect until the clouds won out and the sky turned dark.

With sleep-deprived steps I made my way up the long flight of stairs to the second floor. At the end of a little-traveled corridor one finds the oak-finished room that houses the Shoichi Noma Reading Room of the Oriental Division. Often I have come to this spot to read the newspaper or write a letter, but today I was glad to have a legitimate reason to pull some of the volumes from the shelves.

Inside this small chamber sit two long wooden tables, each encircled by a dozen or so chairs. Bookshelves dominate each wall, from floor to the incredibly high ceiling, broken around the room's perimeter by a second-story landing. Librarians staff a desk to the left of the door and upon request retrieve special manuscripts from an adjoining but restricted area. The librarians are themselves members of the ethnic groups represented in this collection. Indian, Japanese, Chinese, and so on. The day I speak of, a woman wearing a purple Muslim head scarf sat behind the desk, reading a large, intricately illustrated book. She did not glance up at me as I entered the room, and I leaned close enough to see that her text was written in Arabic.

Only two other people occupied the room, a young Asian woman and an older African man. As I mentioned earlier, I fancy myself a student of the dynamics of public space, and the way these two had positioned themselves sparked my curatorial impulses. To reiterate, the room holds two long tables, each approximately fifteen feet long and four feet wide. An aisle of say five feet separates them, therefore you might understand why it puzzled me that the woman and the man had planted themselves on the same side of the same table, albeit at opposite ends. If the scene were captured in a still life, critics would surely point out the gross compositional imbalance. I paused in the mouth of the aisle and studied the picture. Which one, I wondered, had arrived first, and which chose to topple the room's balance?

To the outsider it must seem like a small matter. Perhaps it's the fact that I was raised in New York City, where maintaining an appropriate distance in public areas is such an important part of one's psyche. Anyone who has ever walked along Fifth Avenue at rush hour, tried to hail a cab on a rainy Friday night, or angled for an unimpeded view of a famous painting in a crowded museum knows what I'm talking about. Space is a valuable commodity for the urban dweller. Relying on a batlike sonar to navigate the streets, we are obsessed with proportion. We instantly identify and compensate for improper spacing in elevators, theater queues, or on crowded street corners while waiting for the light to change. With every step we enforce a kind of spatial golden mean.

The country bumpkin says, "Give me wide open spaces."

He is repulsed by crowds, period. But in the city we are flexible. There is no single guiding principle to abide by. Our definition of the claustrophobic is constantly tested. We're never really alone, be it on a crowded subway platform, in a quiet library, or even locked inside our apartments. Someone is always around the next corner, making noise outside our windows. To keep from going insane, we teach ourselves to filter. We selectively blind ourselves to protect against the city's continual barrage. And therein lies the paradox. As urbanites, two of our most basic survival instincts stand in conflict to one another. On the one hand, we're acutely sensitive to the smallest details of human interaction. On the other, we have to blot those details out.

Like the librarian before them, the couple in the Shoichi Noma Reading Room simply filtered me out of existence, and that afforded me enough time to contemplate the psychological impact of each remaining seat. I had to act quickly, for in a matter of seconds that other impulse would take over and they'd sense they were being watched. Initially, I felt compelled to plop myself down right in between them and wait for their reaction. What a sight it would have been! The three of us in a row, facing the other empty table like a panel of unemployed judges. Confrontation, however, was not my wish, and a more sensible design came to mind. I turned to the left and deposited my briefcase directly in the center of the neglected table, so that I faced my fellow scholars. The three of us sat equidistant from one another, forming a perfect isosceles triangle. A refreshing balance now presided over the place, but my shrewd maneuver was lost on the other two. Not once did they so much as glance up from their books.

The young woman looked to be a college student. She wore brown plastic-framed glasses fitted with what must have been quarter-inch-thick lenses, a sweatshirt with a university insignia, and a green, elastic headband wrapped around her wrist. The title of her book hinted at her probable nationality. *Korean Women of the Twentieth Century*. From time to time she jotted down notes on a spiral pad.

To my right, the man read from a more arcane title. *Life Force*. He wore jeans, a blue denim jacket, and a small knitted skullcap patterned in a colorful blue and green geometric design. His beard was just starting to show traces of gray, and he stroked it with his long index finger and curling thumb. He had a vaguely spiritual presence. An old sage, I thought. An urban preacher. After reading a paragraph or two, he'd close his eyes and take counsel with his thoughts. Then, after a deep breath, he'd return to the page.

There are few places better than the public library to take a good long time to observe people, but today I had more pressing objectives. I unpacked a fresh yellow legal pad and two sharpened pencils, then I scanned the shelves behind me for titles related to India. I did not have to search far. The wall to my left pertained to all things Indian. Customs, economic structure, geography, literature, art, government. I removed several volumes and spread them out on the table. Strangely enough, none of the books gave mention to the tilaka, nor could I find the word in any dictionaries or indexes. Most of them proved quite dry, and I exchanged dozens after reading a sentence or two. On my third such trip back to the shelves, however, I happened upon a slim black volume entitled *Death in Banaras*.

Yes, Maya had been right to scold my ignorance of such an important city, and the more I learned, the more ashamed I felt for not having known earlier. Over the course of the next two hours I sat reading Jonathan P. Parry's anthropological work in a state of total absorption. It took all my powers of concentration to try to make sense of one mysterious passage after the other. Here is just a small example:

Those with the eyes to see know that Kashi (the
ancient spiritual name for Banaras) is both the origin-
point and a microcosm of the universe; that it stands
outside space and time yet all space is contained within
it. . . .

This particular paragraph kept me busy for some time.
Until that day I had only heard art critics talk in such grandiose
terms, but then I must confess that the world of religion is
altogether foreign to me. Both staunch atheists, my parents
were repulsed by the notion that mankind might consider itself
the focal point of the universe. My father often launched into
tirades on the subject. "Guilt," I recall him saying from behind
his newspaper. "That's what religion is all about. People are lost,
and guilt is the way they find rootedness. The world makes no
sense. There is no *why* to it all, no explanation to grip on to, so
human beings created the concept of sin. Do you know what
faith is? An admission of defeat. Faith is what you fall back on
when you're not able to prove a point with hard evidence. Life
is too short for such nonsense. Happiness! You must find a way
to make yourself happy. That's what's important. And you have
to do it yourself. There's no book or guru or preacher who can
do it for you. Is anyone listening to what I'm saying? No, I
thought not."

While I've learned to take what he says about happiness
with a grain of salt, his description of faith and religion always
struck me as on the mark. But I also must confess harboring a
secret yearning for the unexplainable, for a supernatural force.
As a boy, I'd sit awake in bed and ask the gods for traffic
accidents to befall my school-yard enemies, to put spells on the
girls so that they'd find me irresistible. For a time, voodoo dolls
held a special fascination, but after a few failed attempts with
stolen T-shirts, hat pins, and an old teddy bear, I gave up on

them. In part, that may have been what intrigued me so much about Banaras, if I can be so bold as to diagnose my own behavioral motives. At long last I had found a doorway into that hidden world, but could there be any truth to these mystical claims? A city standing outside of time and space. I read on.

Hindus from all over the globe travel to Banaras with the express purpose of dying within its city limits. Everyone who does, it is said, achieves instant "liberation" from his or her earthly sins. Ascension is not categorically denied to those who aren't lucky enough to die or be cremated in Banaras, but it's not assured either.

Though it may sound barbaric, or at the very least macabre, to those of us in the West, it is not an unusual sight to see old men paddle out into the Ganges in little dug-out canoes, fasten ballast to their ankles, capsize their boats, and sink slowly to a silt-bottomed grave. Corpses are also brought in from all over the country and piled up to be burned in one of three crematoria that hug the banks at a bend in the sacred river. Stacks of bodies, thirty or forty high. The pyres churn out a constant stream of black smoke—an asphalt road leading up into the heavens.

Approaching noon, I finally took my eyes away from Mr. Parry's lecture and was shocked to discover that the triangular balance of the room had been shattered. The Asian woman was gone, replaced by a Caucasian man late in his years. This elderly gentleman had chosen to sit in a spot that defied all logic— directly across from the African man. The only possible explanation was that he must have entered while the Asian woman was still there. To crowd the African's space while an entirely empty end of the table lay open went against every rule of public courtesy. Perplexed by the chronology of it all, I lost my ability to concentrate on Banaras. I replaced the books and resolved to come back in a day or two.

Outside, the rain poured down with monsoonlike fury. The streets were two inches deep with water and there wasn't a cab for hire anywhere in sight. Waiting for the squall to pass, I leaned back against one of the marble Corinthian columns and tried to sort out all I had learned about Maya Vanasi's home.

●

M y weekend passed with an ever-heightening sense of anxiety. There had been no word from her, though I don't know why I expected differently. By then she should have recognized the potential dangers of Harlem and moved to a safer address. So shouldn't that merit a phone call? And what if she hadn't moved? The thought of her huddled in a corner of her room after dark gave my stomach a pain. My overactive imagination worked late into the night and spilled over into a relentless series of nightmares. Maya murdered by drug dealers. Maya robbed at knifepoint deep in the northern reaches of Central Park. I couldn't take another six nights of this. I contemplated a phone call but knew that her reassurances would never calm my doubts. No, a firsthand inspection was the only way to be sure of her safety. As is probably obvious, an ulterior motive lay behind my decision—to interact with her as much as possible before my self-imposed exile. The cultural barrier between us left me feeling like I still had a long way to go to understand her.

My taxi driver looked back at me with an apprehensive stare when I gave him the Old Memorial's address. Most cabbies routinely avoid Harlem, outright refusing the fare even though doing so is against the law. I reassured the driver, whose Eastern European consonant-laden name I didn't have a clue how to pronounce, that I would only be a moment and required a return trip downtown. Reluctantly, he agreed and drove on. We wove a ragged stop-and-go path up Eighth Avenue to Columbus Circle and continued north via Central Park West. The trees were in dense bloom, and I enjoyed the view of joggers, Rollerbladers, and mothers pushing baby strollers.

But by the time the park had finished, a different reality lay all too bare. It is only a slight exaggeration to say that the fifteen blocks between the top of the park and One Hundred and Twenty-fifth Street are best described as a war zone. Building after building along Lenox Avenue was either abandoned, bricked up, or burned out. Chain-link fences bordered vacant lots of dirt and crumbling brick. A surreal scene right out of a Hollywood western, the heat of that day was so intense that the horizon appeared to be melting.

We stopped at a light at the corner of One Hundred and Sixteenth Street. I watched in disbelief as a crew of half-naked workmen wielding mere sledgehammers did battle against the façade of an old brownstone. So much for technological progress. The heat-blurred image of the wrecking crew was transfixing, and as the cab continued on, I looked back over my shoulder to make sure I hadn't just imagined it.

Old worn-out men sat slouching on every street corner, some with bottles in bags, some fanning themselves with folded-over newspapers. Everything, every bit of what I saw on that stretch, spoke of desolation and hopelessness, especially in contrast to the wealth and leisure of ten blocks back. One tends to romanticize the place one lives in, glossing over problems and difference with charitable optimism. But here in this stagnant pocket of the city, I was hard put to squeeze out a drop of romance. As I sped through the squalor in the relative safety of my car, a passage from *Death in Banaras* came to mind:

If the heart is good, the Ganges is in the wooden
bowl; if the heart is true, Mecca is in the shit-house.

The saying attempts to explain the apparent contradiction
between Banaras as spiritual center floating untouched by time
and space and Banaras as slum-ridden, decaying city. Put another way: If one doesn't recognize the eternal perfection of
Banaras, then the problem is that of the perceiver. Perhaps the
same was true here in the crumbling ruin of Harlem. Perhaps
the desolation around me was just a mirage. I found myself
chuckling out loud at how absurd the idea sounded. It's one
thing to sit in the privileged comfort of a library and let yourself
be swept up in mystical words, but quite another to attempt to
superimpose them over the everyday world. I pity the person
who tries to convince those workers that they're living in an
illusion, that the sweat on their backs, the rats that scurry past
them on their way home, are anything but real. The cabdriver
looked back in the mirror, probably wishing he never had accepted the fare.

Much to my visual relief, when we turned onto One Hundred and Twenty-fifth Street, the surroundings rebounded
somewhat. A variety of stores lined the streets, women appeared, color returned to the windows of apartment buildings,
and different races shared the same sidewalks without incident.
The Old Memorial was in the middle of the block, wedged
between a fast food sandwich shop and a discount clothing
store. A peeling, hand-painted sign of stenciled red letters hung
above a single glass door. It had been damaged by a blow of
some kind—the wood fractured and splintering—so that the
word "Old" was barely legible.

"This it, sir?" the driver asked.

"Looks like the place. Wait here. I'll be five minutes at the
most, keep the meter running."

"I'll keep the meter running," he echoed.

The hotel's glass door was locked. I pushed the bell and was buzzed in. A thick auburn haze of smoke hovered in the low-ceilinged, dark lobby. A torn poster of a well-endowed woman in a yellow bikini hung on the wood-paneled wall. The calendar below it still showed June 1989, four years out of date. Two plastic pots sat on a wooden coffee table, sprouting drooping plastic tulips wedged into green Styrofoam soil. There were no chairs or couches, not a lounge for lounging. A heavy stillness pervaded that made me incredibly tired.

For a minute I marveled at the room's aesthetic perfection. The reality of the place is what I'm getting at. Every detail in its rightful state. The rich hire interior decorators to strike a mood, theater companies employ set designers, but their results are hopelessly transparent. Bright colors and light used to illicit cheerfulness, and so forth. Here, on the other hand, lay something more organic. Yes, there were decorations, but not in a packaged way. I'm not talking about matters of taste. Taste doesn't account for an out-of-date calendar. The room's design had been born haphazardly and with the barest minimum of thought as to its effect on others. Here was that city beneath a city. The filtered material that most people only rarely acknowledge. Of all the arts, photography has best captured this layer of reality. Yet, even photography can't really compete with the sensation of standing in a place like the Old Memorial lobby. From the start it's a stilted contest. The real wins every time.

An elderly black woman sat on the other side of a scratched-up Plexiglas shield not unlike the kind used in cabs. Puffing away at a newly lit long cigarette, she wore bifocals, two large pearl earrings, and a dirty blond wig.

"Afternoon," she said.

"Good afternoon."

"Help you with somethin'?"

"Yes, I hope so. I'm here to see one of your guests. The name is Ms. Vanasi, Ms. Maya Vanasi."

"Room number?"

"I don't know, she didn't tell me."

"Spell it."

"V-a-n-a-s-i."

She ran her index finger down a list of names on the registry. "Nope."

"No?"

"Nobody here named Vanasi. You sure you got the right hotel?"

"Old Memorial, right?"

"That's right."

"She checked in a week ago. A week ago Tuesday I think."

The woman licked her thumb and peeled back six or seven grimy pages in her ratty old book. It looked like they'd used it for years, erasing and reentering names as their guests came and went. The lobby was dead quiet while I waited, and it was easy to reconstruct the scene depicted in the *Times* article describing the drug bust.

"Taylor, Wilson, Thompson, López," she said, and flipped back another page. "Nope. She's not here. I don't see anybody named Vanasi."

"You're sure?"

"Yes I'm sure." She sounded upset that I might be questioning her competence.

"I'm sorry. You see, it's very important that I find her, and this was the hotel she told me she was staying in."

"Well I don't see it. Don't know what to tell you. If she was here, I'd have the name."

"Perhaps I can describe her for you. She's an Indian woman. Black hair, wears a red dot on her forehead."

"A red dot?"

"You know the kind. A circular red dot right here." I pointed to the spot between my eyebrows.

The old woman pushed her glasses up higher on her nose, picked up a newspaper, and began browsing.

"Excuse me," I said, doing my best to control my temper. "The woman, have you seen her? Perhaps she registered under a different name."

She took a long drag off her cigarette and exhaled the smoke directly at the shield between us. "If you got the right name I'll check, but if you don't there's nothing I can do for you."

"Do you mind if I have a look at the registry?"

She returned to her paper without dignifying my ludicrous question with an answer. Clearly, I wasn't going to get much further. Shouting wouldn't help.

The old woman's indifference maddened me, but more than anything I was simply baffled by the new information. No Maya Vanasi at the Old Memorial? I walked toward the door and the old woman was only too glad to hold down the buzzer for as long as it took for me to be gone.

The bright sun and its afterimage momentarily blinded me as I stepped out onto the sidewalk. I very nearly ran into a young man wearing a leather cap and sagging trousers.

"What's your problem?" he shouted.

I reached for the door of the cab. Maya Vanasi is my problem, I responded in thought. The whereabouts of Maya Vanasi.

No matter where I traveled for the next five days—the real estate office, various art galleries, cafés and restaurants—I could not escape the thought of her. An endless back-and-forth filled my head. I tried to convince myself that the woman at the Old Memorial had simply made a mistake, simply sped past the name on the registry without realizing it, but then, why hadn't she reacted to the physical description? And presuming Maya had indeed switched hotels, why wasn't there any record of her initial visit? Furthermore, why hadn't Maya notified me of the change in case of emergency? My worst and most insistent fear was that she wouldn't show up Monday morning. What then? Presumably my backup girls would have made other plans.

Waiting for a phone call that never came, I spent nearly all of the final seventy-two hours at the rental apartment. I even slept there, which is unusual, as I much prefer the bed and surroundings of my own place. I left only once. A trip to the video store and a stop off at home to check my messages. Henry had called. "I'm in painting mode. Call you in a couple of days. Might have some good news by then."

For the majority of my vigil I planted myself in the armchair and looked up at Degas's "Interior." Never had I studied it, or any other painting for that matter, with such unwavering attention in a single sitting.

Like many of his fellow Impressionists, Degas painted passing moments. Snapshots, snippets of everyday life. Women yawning, a horse and rider passing by, women bathing. But in the process he elevated those fleeting seconds into the classical realm. He was responding to the times, to what he saw as a tyrannical conservatism of what society considered valid subject matter for painting. "Wake up, Paris!" he cried out in his works. "Art is all around you!" That's what people so often forget about the Impressionists, their revolt against the boundaries of convention challenged tradition just as much as any abstract expressionist or Dadaist later would. As I'm writing these words, it's clear how strong an influence Degas's ideas have had on me. Searching out what others overlook. Pushing the limit of where one can find art. These are the very same preoccupations that fill my day.

What's unusual about "Interior" is that Degas chose to paint a scene of greater narrative gravity—the resolution of a novel. But unlike a posed portrait, the characters are depicted in midstream. There is nothing static about the piece. The viewer senses the swift passage of time and is drawn to speculate upon the past, present, and future of the subjects. They are alive. Such was the power of his frame. It immortalized his subjects without stopping time.

As I looked up at the two lovers, I found renewed identification with their sense of loss. We sat together in that glowing room of the imagination, passing the hours one by one. Lame and depleted, we kept each other company. Thinking, mourning, trying to figure out what to do next.

●

I awoke in the armchair at twilight. My neck was stiff and my head throbbed as though I had a hangover. When the night's meditation mutated into full-fledged unconscious dreaming was impossible to pinpoint. I had struck such a deep state of reverie that I didn't recall falling asleep. I got up, stretched, and ran the palm of my hand over my Oxford shirt in an attempt to iron out the wrinkles. Hunger pangs cramped my stomach and I needed a shave. I went to the refrigerator. The California rolls had passed their prime, so I tossed them. Five-thirty. Six and a half hours before Maya's big moment. I buttoned up my shirt and headed home.

Outside, sunlight bounced off puddles and leftover drops of rain on car windshields. It was a blinding display. My mood was dour, and the SoHo streets were empty save for the occasional passing cab. Even in the daylight I'm not completely comfortable on uncrowded streets. I've never understood people who say they feel safer in the country. Some house in the thick woods with no neighbors for miles. I'll take a bustling metropolis any day. I rubbed my tired eyes and stopped for espresso beans at the twenty-four-hour corner store.

The long hours of fantasy and speculation had given way to a strong dose of humility. Friday, Saturday, and Sunday had flown by, and as I looked back upon the lost time, I asked myself what it was about Maya that pulled me down so quickly.

Back in my own apartment, the familiar smell of photographic developer soothed my unsteady nerves. The light on the answering machine blinked, and I pressed the messages button. "It's your mother calling. You remember me, don't you, dear? The one who looked after you all those years. The one who picked out your name. We've just come back from a weekend in Majorca. Lovely. If you need to reach us, we'll be in Marseilles for the next two weeks, then up to Colmar for the hot season. Listen, why don't you get out of that godforsaken city and visit? How can you stand the summer there? Do us a favor and watch the house in Marseilles while we're gone. Though I suppose it's out of the question because of your condition, or whatever it is you're calling it these days. I don't pretend to understand. Why in God's name would someone be afraid of a wide-open view? I know I promised not to talk about it. What else shall I ask you? What do you do with yourself all day long? The only news we ever hear of you comes from the real estate office. Maxwell says you're making a mint, by the way. Congratulations. Your father is fine if not slower. He sleeps so damn much. This summer he's going to take a course on how to make chocolate. Some renowned chef in Colmar. You and your father, always with your little hobbies. He sends his love, of course. There's a camera lens he wants you to try to find for him. I'm sure he'll call with details. Then again, why don't you surprise him and call first? Forgive me. God, I hate the way I must sound. I hate the thought of you hating the way I sound. It's just that as I was dialing I realized it had been a full two months since your last measly postcard. Try and call. Please. I'll say good-bye now. Good-bye. Love and so on."

Mother. I glared down at the machine. Try to understand

her frustration, I tell myself. Five years and I still haven't seen
their new home. Perhaps she feels a tad guilty that her only
child is ill and she's so far away. Father doesn't worry much.
"Happiness! It's what I keep telling you. It boils down to the
question of whether or not you're going to try to make yourself
happy. Everyone has limitations. You just have to teach yourself
how to persevere." I adore his ability to reduce all the complex-
ity of existence into those trite, motivational-plaque–like snippets. He could have written bumper stickers for a living. Never
mind the fact that other people might have differing ideas as to
what constitutes happiness. He speaks in code, Father does.
Working hard for financial reward is what he really means. Per-
severance equals steady paychecks. He's a product of his time,
and I suppose I forgive him.

What I refuse to take in good humor, on the other hand, is
my mother's skeptical, superior tone. After all, it was her therapist who diagnosed me. My condition—wait, scratch that. *Condition* is a word that gives it too much status. My problem, or
intermittent problem—that's not right either. Whatever the
correct term, it refers to a bizarre derivation of what doctors of
the mind refer to as agoraphobia, or, the fear of open spaces.
The very opposite of a claustrophobic, my symptoms arise from
having too much emptiness in front of me.

I first noticed it just after graduating Columbia business
school. My father and I attended an outdoor cocktail party atop
the World Trade Center with a few dozen civic leaders, develop-
ers, philanthropists, and press people. We stepped out onto the
gusty observation deck. The view was magnificent. A clear sky,
an enormous sky, the horizon looked as though it stretched out
to Pennsylvania. A swift and sharp jolt of nausea hit me. My
mouth flooded with saliva. The mayor was giving a speech. I
discovered I couldn't move. My shaking knees started to give

way. My father was whispering to a colleague. Suddenly, I doubled over and threw up. The crowd fanned out away from me. A painfully embarrassing moment.

"Must just be a case of vertigo," my father hastened to assure the disturbed onlookers. "Excuse us, please. He'll be all right." He put his arm around my waist and led me back inside the sheltered stairwell, where, just like that, the sickness dissipated.

"But he's never had a fear of heights before," my mother said when we got back home. "Maybe there's something wrong with him."

"Why do you have to say it as though it were his fault?"

"You know that's not what I meant."

"We were on the tallest building in the world, Harriet. You'd have to be crazy not to get sick. I felt queasy myself. Besides, he says he's fine."

"He is obviously not fine. I think he should get treatment. I'll call Dr. Wasserstrom."

"I'm fine, Mother. I don't need a shrink."

A whole ten months passed before my next episode. It was the same year I started the apartment project. My parents had just moved abroad, and my father called and asked if I'd inspect some real estate he was interested in upstate. I rented a car. As I drove across the George Washington Bridge, I realized it was the first time I'd been outside of the city in two years. Time has a way of sneaking past you in New York, because every day is so packed full.

Perhaps the snug confines of the compact car shielded me from the symptoms, because the long view up the brownish-green Hudson River didn't cause me any discomfort. I turned north onto the Palisades Parkway, admiring the woods and rolling hills as I went. A road sign advertised a scenic overlook. Being in no particular hurry, I exited, and pulled into a parking spot facing the banks of the river. I got out of the car, and walked toward a circular lookout point landscaped with boulders and shrubs. I rounded a thicket of oak and maple trees and came into the totality of the view—the river, the drab row houses in the town of Yonkers in the distance, the pale blue sky. Nausea kicked me in the gut, and I struggled to catch my breath. A cold sweat swept over me. Complete paralysis ensued. I became as helpless as an acrophobic stuck on a ledge.

The humorous part of the story—though I certainly didn't see it at the time—was that right in that most vulnerable state, a squirrel came hopping out of the brush and sat up on his hind legs on the concrete rail in front of me. I guess he'd gotten used to being fed. We stood perfectly still, facing one another, for what felt like an hour. My condition worsened. Short breaths, heart rate racing out of control. A steady crescendo of adrenaline with no foreseeable outlet. The hungry squirrel trotted off. I told myself I was either going to pass out or pop like a ripe aneurysm. But then, by a stroke of pure luck, I happened to close my eyes. Amazingly, the sensation receded. Such a simple solution, it didn't seem right that it should work. Eyes clamped shut, the overwhelming expanse before me disappeared. I turned around and felt my way back to the car. Fearing that I'd suffered a mild heart attack, I sped toward the city and my doctor's office. "A bout of severe anxiety," he said, and scribbled out a prescription for Valium. "You young people work too much. Yuppies, I don't understand this generation. What's the big hurry? You should slow down, enjoy life."

This time my mother insisted I see her therapist. "Listen, these things tend to worsen before they get better," she cautioned in a confident tone that told me she had no idea what she was talking about.

Though I have nothing against the idea of self-analysis per se, I've always shunned formalized therapy. Admittedly, growing up with a mother who took two weekly sessions for as long as I could remember with little or no outward effect may account for my bias. But losing control of my body seemed serious. It truly scared me. Let me say that having a doctor give your condition a name is immensely calming. She could have said cancer and I'd probably have felt better. The not knowing is the terrible part. "How does one cure agora-whatever-it-is?" I asked.

"First, you need to figure out how to live with it. Learn the boundaries."

"No more scenic views?"

"Not for a little while. Tell me, anything you can think of that might have brought this on?"

"Like what?"

"Major life changes perhaps."

"Besides graduating business school and having my parents move across the Atlantic?"

"We could set up regular sessions if you like."

"Cute. Now don't go telling my mother any of this, but I'm ecstatic to be rid of them for a while. Just as happy as I was to finish school. Free at last, God almighty, I'm . . ."

She smiled. "Sometimes freedom is a scary prospect."

"No, no. Don't start in with the palm reading just yet."

"All right. So what *do* you want to do?"

"I'd be quite content if I could simply control the symptoms. Will they get worse?"

"Hard to say. I don't know enough about what it is you may or may not have."

"Well I obviously have something."

"It's not so clear-cut. You have something that sounds similar to a psychological phenomenon. Besides, there's no one way to treat agoraphobia even if that's what you do have. It's like curing a fear of water. There are techniques, but the general rule in fixing this kind of thing is go with whatever works."

"Aren't there any pills you could prescribe?"

"Nothing that'll prevent another episode."

"Learn my boundaries, you say."

"It's a start."

I got back to my apartment and stared out the back windows. Paranoia set in. When would the next attack strike? The three-block view down Sullivan Street was manageable now, but tomorrow? How soon before the disease would turn even the smallest distances against me? I went to the phone and dialed my carpenter. As if bracing myself for an offshore hurricane, I had him board up the windows. Preventive medicine. I would beat this thing before it beat me.

It's funny what consequences stem from adverse situations. The fear of losing my mobility caused me to seal the windows, which in turn gave me the idea to rescue my childhood darkroom equipment from the dust of my parents' crawl space.

Despite the encouragement of my high school photography teacher, Rolph Penn, that I continue on to art school, I turned away from photography when I was eighteen. "Don't get me wrong," my father told me one morning at breakfast, "photography is a lovely hobby. But you've got to think realistically about making a living. I'm offering you a brilliant opportunity. I've worked hard to give you this—too hard—and I'm not going to sit by and watch you miss out because of some adolescent whim. You can always take your pictures on the side."

"I still don't see what the rush is. Why can't I wait a little before I learn the business? Have some time off. Go someplace—I don't know. You're not planning on retiring just yet."

"Three years, maybe four. That's not long in the grand

scheme, and before I do retire I'm going to need to see you apply yourself. I mean really apply yourself. Do you understand? I've got to know that I'll be leaving the firm with a competent leader. A show of good faith, that's what I'm asking."

I entered Columbia the following fall, declaring my major in economics. Looking back, I suppose that if I really had taken a stand, they wouldn't have disinherited me. I could have demanded they send me to art school, but real estate had been so ingrained in me by then it felt more like genetic destiny than a career choice.

So I squeaked by with minimum effort. Earned my bachelor's degree, then trudged on with barely enough steam to pick up an MBA. What reason was there to apply myself? I already understood how it all worked. Buying and selling properties in the greatest, most profitable market in the world doesn't take a great deal of smarts, it takes a great deal of money, which my father had. The strategy is simple. Purchase a building almost anywhere in Manhattan, sit on it until the price goes through the ceiling, then sell. Think long-term and you can't lose.

Columbia's art history department more than sustained me throughout my college years. To this day, my parents are still clueless about this side of their only son. They know only a fraction of me, but it's probably just as well. Art is to them a mere diversion from their beloved money-making grind. At its best, it's a risky investment.

In between courses on micromanagement and macroeconomics, I sat in on lectures on cubism, painting from the medieval period, and Impressionism. I devoured the library's massive collection. From the cave paintings at Lascaux to the most vulgar contemporary films, I set about memorizing the time line of Western art. Then it was out into the city, to every gallery and museum show I could find. Dan Flavin, Donald Judd, Jasper Johns, Cindy Sherman.

The early-eighties art scene sped along at a breakneck pace. I look back on it as a messy assault on form. Painting fell into disrepute. Sculpture filled the void. Video hit the scene. With the rise of conceptualized art, pretty things lost their importance. The guiding impulse of the time seemed to be to tear down, to criticize by using as much irony as possible. And yet, amid the entropy, a logical direction became apparent. One by one the boundaries that separated an artistic work from the everyday world started vanishing. Art was merging with real life—a welcome development as far as I was concerned. Soon, I assured myself, we wouldn't be able to tell the two apart.

Which brings me back to the story of the darkroom set. I assembled it in my newly blackened spare bedroom and was struck by a daunting question. It was all very well for me to diagnose the current state of the art world, but how did I hope to add to the cacophony? What was there to take pictures of that hadn't already been done a thousand times? Here again, a good turn arose from the bad, and for the first time I came to see the agoraphobia as a blessing. The fact that the new baffles kept others from looking in inspired me to drill the hole and start looking out. In that subversive act I found the creative boundary not yet crossed. Surveillance.

That first view from the hole wasn't anything to get excited over. I gazed out at the same empty five-story building that had been there my whole life. "Probably a tax writeoff," my father once observed. But fate seemed to bolster me at every turn, because the very next month a For Sale sign appeared on the façade. With Father's blessing I bought the property and began a full renovation.

"One more thing about the new place," I explained to him over the crackle of a bad overseas connection. "I'd like to be responsible for renting the units."

"What do you mean? Speak up, I can't hear you very well."

"I said I'd like to pick the people. I'll do the search my-self."

"But that's what we pay Maxwell for."

"It'll be a good learning experience. Besides, I feel respon-sible. I want it to be perfect, top to bottom."

"Well, then I leave it in your hands." I could tell from his tone how proud he was that I seemed to have finally taken to the family business. Ever since then I've kept myself cloistered in Manhattan, and all without a further bout of agoraphobia.

Maya's first day. I went to the bookshelf and took a moment to look through the large red photo albums that I've filled with pictures of the four women before her. They were immensely reassuring. Claire, Victoria, Laura, and Paula. No, I told myself, Ms. Vanasi had not been the first, nor would she be the last. Years from now she'd be just another two-dimensional chapter in my life's work.

After showering, I prepared myself an espresso and put Stravinsky's "Rite of Spring" on the stereo at an appropriately soaring volume. I dressed in casual cotton slacks and a short-sleeve shirt, an outfit comfortable for a long plane ride. Then I stuffed my travel duffel full of dirty laundry and assembled an impressive-looking camera bag. I dialed the limousine service and gave the address for the rental apartment and a one-thirty P.M. pickup time. On the way out, I took the two videos I had rented the day before, then slung the bags over my shoulder.

Sweat beaded on my brow by the time I reached the front door of the other building. I struggled up the stairs, but now that I was taking action again, I felt chipper. Inside the apartment I assembled my bags in a pile next to the front door, then placed the videos atop the living room television.

Time for one last double-check. First, the kitchen. Fridge and trash emptied. Cupboards clear. To the bedroom. In the

nightstand drawer I keep a single paperback for bedtime reading, an anonymous work entitled *My Secret Life*. It's the story of
a man's clandestine sexual escapades in Victorian England. Now
that I think about it, I see that the book served as part of the
inspiration to put my own story into words. Like the author of
My Secret Life, I haven't kept any secrets from these pages.
Still, I'm careful to tell the story in a patient and detailed manner so as to guard against misinterpretation. I'm not writing for
anyone in particular, but the artifice of an audience has proven
helpful in gaining perspective. Perhaps that's the thin line that
will always distinguish art from everyday life. Artists envision
the effect of their output on other human beings. Even someone like Joseph Cornell, sitting in his solitary barn making those
delicate boxes. Though he may never have intended showing
them to another soul, he most certainly supposed an audience.
Some have said all art stems from vanity, but a truer self-
absorption would be to create without considering anybody
else. It seems to me that making art always was and will be an
act of communication, whether or not the creation ever reaches
its imagined audience.

I flipped open the paperback to one of my favorite passages, in which the hero seduces a reluctant maidservant, and
inserted the yellow bookmark. Depending on the personality of
my boarder, I select different sections. Nothing scientific, just a
hunch as to what they might find intriguing.

I took a peek at myself in the freestanding, full-length
mirror that resides between the nightstand and the closet to
make sure it was positioned correctly—so that it threw its reflection back toward the window. The bedroom closet must
have an organized look to it. Four or five old suits, a half dozen
pairs of shoes, top three drawers of the clothes chest cleared
out. Plenty of space for her to store her things.

The hall closet, on the other hand, is jammed to capacity. My tenant should think of this as the place I've hastily thrown my clutter. Among the items I store there are a file cabinet, ironing board, winter coats, snow boots, squash racquet, extra down-comforter, and, most important, the locked metal box of "personal" items, the contents of which I'll discuss later. I'm going for a scattered feel here.

Ten o'clock. The waiting started getting to me. I realized I hadn't eaten, so I popped over to l'Esperance and sat at an outdoor table. It was a magnificent day. Clear skies, seventy degrees, low humidity. I gobbled down a cheese danish and sipped Lapsang souchong tea. This would be the last time that summer for Jefferson to enjoy a SoHo café, assuming Maya showed up. I let out a sigh and told myself to enjoy the weather.

A second later I caught sight of my friend Henry rumbling down the street with his Cro-Magnon gait. He's a huge individual. Six foot four, and over two hundred pounds of pure bulk. The art-barbarian, I call him. He pays no mind to his outward appearance, rarely bothers to shave, and never combs his hair. At twenty-four years old, it's all part of his bohemian fantasy of what an artist is supposed to look like, and he acts the part well. "Slow down, my friend, you're going to hurt somebody at that speed."

"What are you doing here?" he asked. "Isn't it the first of the month?"

"Sit down, have a drink."

"No time. I'm meeting a gallery owner for breakfast."

"Which gallery?"

"Archer-Handsforth. Show coming up on the fifteenth."

"The fifteenth of when?"

"This month."

"Jesus Christ, Henry!"

"What? What's the matter? I told you—"

"No, Henry, you certainly did not."

"Left you a message. Maybe your machine is broken."

"My machine works fine. I just checked it."

"Well now you know."

"How long will it run?"

"Only three weeks."

"Three weeks! Are you crazy, Henry? Are you hearing yourself? Which paintings? Not Paula. Tell me you're not showing Paula."

"Would you please stop worrying? I'm showing Victoria."

"You finished Victoria?"

He rocked back and forth on his heels and smiled.

"When did this happen? Why didn't you call me? Henry, that's wonderful, but you can't just show the paintings in a gallery before I have a chance to look at them."

"The Victoria series is different. Very blurred, practically abstract."

"I am familiar with your painting, Henry. One thing you don't do is abstraction."

"Maybe you aren't listening to what I'm saying. This is Archer-Handsforth we're talking about, not some lousy East Village café."

"I'm happy for you, Henry. Don't think I'm not, but please don't forget our arrangement."

"Nothing to worry about. I'm telling you, they could have been painted anywhere. I'll show them to you. You'll see."

I poured some more tea and added a fresh lemon twist to the cup. "Henry, let me ask you something. You do realize who shows work in the summer?"

"Go ahead, tell me. Who shows work in the summer?"

"Artists who can't get a show in the fall. This isn't a good career move, I'm warning you. You'll be labeled, falsely of course, but labeled nonetheless."

We looked away from each other. He wouldn't be swayed from showing the paintings. I really didn't blame him, an Archer-Handsforth show couldn't be sneezed at, regardless of the season. I trusted his discretion, just had to make sure he understood my sensitivity.

"You are still subletting, right?" he asked.

"Why do you think I'm so upset?"

"Don't be. Tell me about the new girl?"

"I think you'll be pleasantly surprised."

"That's what you always say."

"Do I?"

"Yes, you do."

"But I mean it this time, and I know how that sounds, but it's true. I'm talking about a whole new realm, a whole other category."

"Heard it before. You said the same thing about Paula."

"Thank you very much, Henry, but as a matter of record, that is not exactly what I said about Paula. 'She's something special' were my words. I never said 'new realm' or 'whole other category' or anything of the sort. We're in for a surprise. I can feel it. It's going to be new."

"You know what you are? You're a kid. A little kid waiting in line at a roller coaster. Totally overexcited."

"Henry, I find it a bit disturbing that you, nearly seven years my junior, should compare me to a spoiled child."

"My God, a whole seven years!"

"That's a lot in the twenties. It's a time of great changes."

He smiled. "No, what you find disturbing is the fact that I'm right." He checked his watch. "I'm late. Call me tomorrow. I'll be home after five, and stop worrying."

"Be careful, Henry. Please, for both our sakes."

He tipped his baseball hat and went along his way. Showing the paintings was a risk, but for the moment I put my mind at ease. I was glad to learn that I wasn't acting out of the ordinary with Maya. Perhaps I did get this bent out of shape about all of them.

●

As precise as any alarm clock, the buzzer rang just as the grandfather clock chimed twelve. I was overcome with relief. "Maya?" I called into the intercom.

"Yes, it is me."

I listened at the open door for the sound of her footsteps just as I had on our first meeting. Strange, but this time I heard the distinct slap of leather sole against linoleum for each and every stair along the way. She rounded the corner beaming her beautiful smile, and I was struck with another difference. No red dot on her forehead. Yet her face maintained its peaceful balance; perhaps I'd given the third eye too much credit the first time we'd met. "It's good to see you," I said. "Where are your bags?"

"I'll fetch them later."

"Are you hungry?"

"Starving."

"Maybe we should go eat first. Then I can give you one last run-through."

"Yes, let's eat. Do you know a good place?"

"I know just about all of them."

We sat on the patio at Fleur de Lis amid the flowering rhododendron and rosebushes.

"This seems to be a very expensive restaurant," she said, eyeing the menu.

"Don't worry, my treat. It's the least I could do after letting you stay in a place as bad as the Old Memorial all these nights."

"Thank you," she replied. I came very close to confronting her about the hotel, but held my tongue. Why? I ask myself. All week I'd been waiting to find out where she had really been. It's difficult to describe it, but talking to her had a strange effect on me. I waited for her every word. I turned passive, watchful. Normally, language is my strong suit in this type of situation. I'm always the aggressor, employing humor to smooth over awkward silences. Perhaps the cultural gap had something to do with it, but I no longer trusted my own jokes. The silence built for an unbearable duration. I didn't know how to begin. Though I'd mapped out the conversation a hundred times beforehand, I was as lost as an unprepared understudy thrust onstage as the curtain rises. Finally, I couldn't stand it any longer. "Tell me, how was it staying there?"

"Perfect. Not one complaint."

"Really?"

"Yes," she said with a smile.

"Glad to hear it." Could the receptionist have made a mistake after all? "May I ask another question?"

"Why not?"

I pointed between my eyebrows. "The tilaka. You're not wearing it today."

"Because I have not applied the mark does not mean that the bindi does not exist."

"Bindi?"

"Another word for you to learn."

"The same as tilaka?"

"Some mornings I am lazy. But the third eye is eternal. It

need not be recognized with pigment every moment. Do you
know the teachings of the Bhagavad Gita?"

"The book? Yes, I've heard of it, though I can't say I've
ever read it."

"One of my favorite parts, let me see if I can remember,
Krishna tells Arjuna . . . 'Feelings produced from contact
with the senses are transitory, have a beginning and an end. But
the self is never born, nor does it die.' "

"That's pretty good. One more time."

She repeated the passage.

"Do you mind if I take a stab at what it might mean?" I
asked.

"Please do."

"Something having to do with permanence. That the permanent state of things, or the way things really are, might not be
gotten at through the senses?"

"Something like that."

"Reminds me of Plato. He was always going on about how
you couldn't trust what you saw. And the third eye represents
the self, is that it?"

"I wasn't quite finished."

"Sorry."

"The self isn't born nor does it die. The next line is something like . . . 'Having been, the self never falls into a state of
nonbeing. It is never destroyed even when the body is destroyed.' "

"So you're speaking metaphorically? Don't judge a book by
its cover. Is that it?"

She smiled politely.

"Of course, I'm over my head here. I don't mean to trivial-
ize." I looked at the bare spot on her forehead. If there was a
window to the soul there, it was made of opaque glass. "I did
some reading on Banaras. Fascinating place, I gather."

"New York isn't so bad either."

I laughed. We ordered lunch. I made sure to avoid beef, opting instead for the broiled monkfish. She chose the poussin. "And wine," I suggested. "You do drink wine, don't you?"

"I prefer red, if that's all right."

"La Crema Pinot Noir," I told the waiter. "So, Maya, you're enjoying New York? Finding your way around all right?"

"How do you Americans say it? A piece of cake. The grid formation makes it very easy. I keep meaning to get to the museums, but I find the streets fascinating. So much life."

"That's my favorite part too. I tend to think of Manhattan as an enormous living museum. I could people-watch the whole day through and never get bored."

"And the Central Park!"

"Magnificent, isn't it? Have you met anyone? Do you have friends?"

"Just this week I met a couple who own an art gallery near here. Very friendly people. They have given me tours of the city and their country house in the Hamptons of Long Island."

"What are their names? Perhaps I know their gallery."

"Stephen Archer and Dianne Handsforth."

An incredible coincidence. "Don't know them," I replied.

"You must go sometime. The artists are of a superior quality. An art lover such as you would surely think so."

"Am I an art lover?"

"You love Degas."

"That's true."

"Just last night I was remembering your painting. It caused me a terrible bout of insomnia. I hope that I won't be so sad every time I look at it."

"Sad?"

"Very much. Don't you find it so?"

"Yes, I do. The tragedy, the subject matter. You know the context?"

"I'm only speaking of what I saw. The look on their faces, such remorse. But that's the curse of a true work of art, it tends to move one."

"You'll get used to it." My mind was itching. Some period of time the night before, both Maya and I reflected upon "Interior." Not to mention Archer-Handsforth. I had to call Henry as soon as possible.

"Do you feel all right?" she asked.

Back at the apartment Maya handed me an envelope filled with both months rent in cash. "Thank you. Unfortunately, I'll be impossible to reach for most of my trip. I can't imagine that you'll have any problems. If you do have an emergency, contact the super. His number is on the refrigerator. I have a message service, so I shouldn't get any calls here, and I've also ordered a hold on my mail. Really there's nothing for you to take care of except—"

"The plants."

"Except the plants." We walked into the living room. "Feel free to use the VCR. There's a decent rental shop two blocks away on Sullivan—oh fuck!" I picked up the cassettes lying on top of the television. "Excuse my language. I forgot to return these. What time is it?"

"Nearly one-thirty."

"My car should be here any moment."

"If you like, I can drop them off."

"Could you? They're paid for through tomorrow. Just put them in the return slot. That would be a big help."

"Gladly."

"Let's see. What am I forgetting? Plants, keys, noise, VCR, super's number. One thing—" I paused and tried to look pensive.

"What is it?"

"Feel at home. The place is yours for the next two months, but if I can just ask you not to use the hall closet. I don't have a lock for it. I trust you, not that there's anything particularly valuable inside, just . . ."

"I understand. The bedroom closet will be more than sufficient for my things."

"Thank you. Well, Maya, I guess that's everything. Any questions?"

"All is clear."

"I'm glad it is." I hesitated for a second. "Tell me, about the tilaka, was I way off with that book-by-its-cover comment?"

"No, not way off."

The buzzer sounded. "I'll be right down," I called. "Have a great time getting to know the city, and take care. I'll see you in two months. Maybe we can talk more then." I held out my hand and she shook it with a good firm grip.

"I hope the photographs turn out to your liking."

"They will." I gathered my bags and winked at her. The look in her eyes caught me off guard. She gave me a calm, penetrating stare, and for a second I feared she could read my thoughts. Then she turned and closed the door.

●

A black Lincoln with tinted windows waited by the curb. The trunk was open, and the driver sat inside just as I had instructed. I placed my bags in the trunk and took a last glance up at the window before getting in the car. She was up there all right, peering down at me, and waved when our eyes met.

"Good day, sir," the driver said in a thick Irish accent.

"Afternoon. I take it they've explained the route?"

"They have. I don't believe I've ever had such a short fare in all my years driving." The car rolled on to the corner and made a left turn.

"I bet not. Trying to impress a girl. You understand."

"Say no more, sir. Happy to help where I can. Yes, I'm always happy to aid in the pursuit of love."

"Thank you." We made another left at the next corner.

"What was the address then, sir?"

"Just ahead here. You can let me off behind the blue van." I pulled a twenty-dollar bill from my pocket and handed it forward. "Keep the change, and could you pop the trunk?"

"Thank you, sir. The name is Gregory. Anytime you need my assistance, please ask for me specifically."

"Will do, Gregory."

My adrenaline was pumping on the elevator ride up to my loft. How I adored this ripened moment, knowing that all the pieces were in place and all that was left was to look and appreciate. I parked the elevator outside my fifth-floor apartment.

Inside I selected Dvořák's Trio in F Minor, Opus 65 as background music, and pushed play on the CD machine. "To the looking glass," I mumbled. The texture of piano, violin, and cello set the perfect mood for observation as I walked to the other side of the floor-through. I have speakers installed on both ends of the long apartment so that Dvořák waited for me in the small front room that I use as observation post and darkroom. I closed the door behind me and shut myself in blackness. My eyes quickly located the sliver of light where a small hole cut into the boarded-up window surrounds my high-powered telephoto lens. Shuffling forward six steps, I caught my toe against the leg of the tripod, felt for the camera body, then found the eyepiece. I steadied myself and dove in.

The windowpane, the dracaena, the bed beyond, and full-length mirror in the corner. One by one they went in and out of focus as I adjusted the depth of field. To repeat, the full-length mirror faces the street, and I know right where to look in it to find the small reflective circle that is my camera's lens. No sign of Maya. I slid the body of the camera to the second preset position on my tripod. The living room. Videos still atop the television, a distorted sidelong view of "Interior." The hall light was on, but I still couldn't see very far into the foyer. The kitchen and the bathroom are blind areas, so it was possible she was in either one. Breath drawn, I waited for what felt like an eternity, panning back and forth from room to room, but she never appeared.

I stepped out of the room for some air and discovered that half an hour had passed. Then I remembered her fascination with the bathtub and rushed back to the eyepiece, hoping I might catch her drying off. After another twenty minutes I went out to the kitchen and poured myself some mineral water. The music stopped, but I was too flustered to pick another composer. I returned for another hour of fruitless searching. By five o'clock my temples ached and my eyes were dry and itching. It infuriated me that I'd wasted so much time looking at empty rooms, but on the other hand, I knew I was getting nearer to the moment when she'd return to the apartment.

How had she slipped away so quickly? After seeing her in the window, my limousine ride lasted all of two minutes. Another two minutes maximum for me to ride the elevator, lock the door, put on music, and walk to the camera. Why had she left so close on my heels? Just another mystery of Maya to add to my list.

I sat down on the couch and tried to clear my head. Think back, I told myself. Maybe this isn't so strange.

When I first began the experiment in 1984, I had five beautiful unfurnished apartments. Five empty frames. I ran an ad in the *New York Times.*

> Sparkling 1 BR, Prime SoHo,
> A/C FP, Mod. Kit., Hrdwd. Flrs.,
> View, $300 per month.
> Call Jefferson, (212) 496-3715.

I faithfully adhered to the first rule in property-renting—find a stable tenant for the long haul. The less traffic and changeover, the better. I wanted realism in all its mundane glory, and that required day-to-day observation over a prolonged period of time. Just like every other landlord in the city, I based my criteria for the tenants on an ability to pay the rent, mental stability, cleanliness, and a promise of courtesy toward one's neighbors. In short, the ideal tenant was someone who'd be next to invisible. The first five to fit the bill were in. Back then, the random quotient seemed an essential part of the piece, and I wanted to study my subjects in as natural an environment as possible.

I selected Mrs. Adolfo for the fourth floor. A fifty-three-year-old wealthy widow, she's all cigarettes, scotch, and romance novels. Her grandchildren come to visit every so often, and she has a bridge game on Tuesdays. Thrilling stuff.

The Seymores, a middle-aged professional couple, live on the third. I wonder if they're not part vampire, as they keep the shades permanently drawn. Just plain bad luck on my part. I see them coming and going and have memorized their drab selection of office outfits.

Zachary Robbins, a fat contractor in his forties, resides on two, but here the sight lines get tight. I can't see very deep into his apartment, and what I have seen doesn't impress me much. Constant television-viewing. I often wonder how many hundreds of jobs he has started throughout the city and left half finished in favor of *General Hospital.*

Sandra Barton rents the ground floor, but she's a flight attendant and is rarely home. Because of the angle, when she is home she has to stand flush against the window before I can see her. Forty-three, single. Hangs plants in her front window, which she's very good at killing. Takes her a day or two after she arrives home before she replaces the dead ones with new victims.

The prized viewing floor is five, because it's on an even plane with my own apartment. Stuart Davis, a lawyer from Virginia, lived in five from 1984 until 1989. I grew to know him as intimately as a roommate. His laundry detergent, Tide, his magazine subscriptions, *The New Yorker, Playboy,* and *Rolling Stone.* His Cheerios. The same cereal every goddamn morning for four and a half years! He'd carry the bowl out from the kitchen and gaze through the window as he ate, as though planning an action-packed day. Nothing could have been further from the truth. He was a true loner. I don't think that in all his tenure on the fifth floor I ever saw him bring anyone home other than his kid brother, whose resemblance I immediately recognized. The exact same John Denver wire-frame glasses and bowl haircut. They looked less like brothers than members of the same geekish cult.

The two of them got hooked on the video game craze, but it was his younger brother who tired of it first. For a time I think I felt sorry for Stuart. "Get out of the damn house!" I'd yell as I watched him fritter his weekend nights away pushing Ms. Pac-Man around the screen before jerking off to *Playboy*. Not that I've got anything against masturbation, but every Friday and Saturday! And always *Playboy*. Use your imagination, man! The corner kiosk sells hundreds of more exciting magazines. Try a foot fetish on for size.

As the years wore on, I grew hateful of his lazy, self-defeating routines. Watching him depressed me, but in part I, too, had grown addicted to the repetition. Something had to give. Though pornography wasn't my initial aim, I couldn't help wishing that just one of the tenants was physically attractive.

I got the call on a Saturday morning. Stuart had accepted a job in Tampa. "I'm sorry to have to give you such short notice, I didn't know the position would start so fast. I need to leave by the end of the week. That gives you a little while before the first. I hope it's enough time. I guess I could help pay part of June's rent—"

"No. Don't worry." I interrupted. "That's wonderful. When can I get in there to paint?"

"The movers come Friday." He sounded almost disappointed that I didn't give him a hard time. "So, it's okay then?"

"Of course. Congratulations!"

After redoing the floors and painting, I placed my ad in the *Times*. On Saturday, June 25, 1989, I conducted the first interview. A young, attractive blond girl named Claire walked through the door. She wore cut-off shorts, a paint-speckled T-shirt, and flip-flop sandals that showed off her fire-engine-red toenails. She smacked away at a piece of bubble gum, a habit I find especially antisocial. Chewing with one's mouth open is bad enough at a dinner table.

The apartment smelled of fresh white paint, and the floors were still a bit tacky from the drying polyurethane. Our conversation reverberated in the empty living room. Despite the gum, she spoke clearly, and she gave off an aura of shyness that made me like her. "I'm only here for the summer. Taking classes at NYU. I know it's probably not what you had in mind, but would it be possible to sublet?"

Instinctively, I started to explain that I needed someone on a permanent basis, but then stopped mid-sentence. It was so perfect. A few months and then on to the next, like an art gallery with rotating exhibitions. How could I have neglected the obvious potential for so long? "But there's no furniture," I said. "Where would you sleep?"

"I can buy a futon. I don't need much. Just a place to rest my head at night and study."

"You will be careful with the bubble gum. I can't have any spots on this floor."

"Very careful. You can trust me. I'll keep the apartment totally clean. You won't be able to tell the difference when I move out, I promise."

Art is often described as a process, an evolution, and with Claire I was still figuring it out, still learning what I was after. Because of her physical beauty and the fact that she'd be there only a short time, I thought I wouldn't grow tired of looking at her. Wrong again.

She never really settled in to her new home, in part because of the emptiness. With nothing to look at besides her books and futon, she stared out the window for long periods of the day. As a result, the photos of her turned out looking terribly static. Girl reading. Girl sleeping. Girl daydreaming. Feeling bored and detached from my subject, I found myself in the same predicament I'd started with. Realism took me only so far. I came to realize that mere observation wasn't enough to fulfill my artistic appetite. I needed greater interaction.

When her summer session ended and she left the apartment, I started searching out furniture at the Broadway and Chelsea flea markets. I created the new environment from scratch, an installation, if you will. Emphasizing comfort, I decided on a more conservative decorative scheme than the one in my own home. Ornate golden picture frames, dark wood furniture, a deep couch with lots of throw pillows, a leather recliner, tasteful Persian rugs throughout, and a queen-sized bed with mahogany headboard. I filled the closets with used clothes and sporting goods bought from the Salvation Army and stoop sales.

Having decided to cast myself in a more central role of the apartment drama, my character quickly took shape. To divert suspicion, I let the other tenants stay put. That way I wouldn't have a building full of beautiful subletters comparing observations about the building. The story about the Guatemalan rain forest came about by chance. After setting up the television and VCR, I turned them on and a nature special materialized on the screen. "Eyes of the Hunter: The Central American Jaguar." Too perfect.

For the next three years the project proceeded along beautifully. Unlike Maya, each of the tenants lay waiting for me by the time I made it to the camera lens. I caught Laura in the act of watching the videos—a disgusted sneer on her face. Victoria stared out the window to admire her new view. For a second I feared that she made out the filtered but still partially reflective circle of my camera lens, but then she turned, plopped on the bed, and took a nap. Paula thrilled me most of all, for without hesitation she started digging in the forbidden hall closet. She even brought the metal box to the bed and tried to pick the lock with a hairpin. If nothing else, the variations in their stories reminded me that one shouldn't attempt to predict the future based solely on the actions of the past.

Victoria! I'd almost forgotten. I picked up the phone and called Henry's studio. His machine answered, and I told him to report in at once. He'd either have to cancel his show at the gallery or substitute other work. There wouldn't be any Victorias, Lauras, Paulas, or Claires hung on the walls of Archer-Handsforth this summer. I told myself not to be angry with him. He had no way of knowing that Maya would become friends with the gallery owners. Unlucky coincidence.

To kill time, I picked up the Arts and Leisure section of the paper and read a glowing review of a new show at the Modern museum. An installation by Cecilia Muñoz, a sculptor who practices what the critic called "self-portraiture, in the metaphoric sense." The materials of the current show consisted of by-products, or representations thereof, of the human body. Hair, fingernails, and feces, to name three.

She was dabbling in that tricky arena of the antiaesthetic. The article quoted Ms. Muñoz as saying ". . . aesthetic pleasure doesn't exist on its own, we create it. What passes for beauty in our society is nothing more than a set of arbitrary associations." When I read her words, I knew she must be a pretty woman. The less-desirable among us know that there's no rewriting beauty and attraction, try though we may. Yes, the human brain has the power to see artistic merit in practically anything it chooses, but that doesn't mean people aren't ulti-mately bound by a more fundamental set of aesthetic truths. Tomorrow I'd see the show and decide for myself. Perhaps I could even convince archrepresentationalist Henry to come along.

Seven o'clock. Back to the window. Twilight descending and still no sign of her. I reset the aperture. The idle waiting was becoming too much to endure. My stomach grumbled with hunger. Refusing to be held a captive any longer, I went to the bathroom and opened the steamer trunk that contains my alter ego for summer. A simple yet effective disguise consisting of a long brown beard, spectacles fitted with glass lenses, and five changes of clothes. Made entirely of human hair, the beard is of the highest professional quality. The glasses are large on my face and hug close to the skin. The thick black frames are especially transformative. The getup makes me look a good ten to fifteen years older. I wonder how much older Maya thought my voice and elocution made me sound? The concept behind the clothing is simply to present myself in a way that Jefferson would not. In a word, slovenly. Coveralls, sweat suits, jeans with holes in the knees, scuffed-up combat boots.

A mere fifteen minutes later I emerged onto the streets of New York a new citizen. I pulled a baseball cap down on my head so that the brim rested just above my brow. The air was sticky, the streets wet from a short burst of rain and crowded with people. Maya could have been anywhere. In a shop, rounding the next corner, sitting in a restaurant, but she wouldn't recognize me. I had learned my part to perfection, even affecting a slight limp. When I put the costume on, I became that other being, one of the anonymous masses that passes by in a blur, real and totally untouchable.

Food. I was thinking Thai—spring rolls and citrus beef salad, but the smell that hit me as I approached Il Teatro stopped me in my tracks. Italian it was.

●

To pen this account of Maya is an odd experience. It represents the first written record in the history of my experiment, as the other cases required little retrospection. The need
to write is the need to clarify, and, to my surprise, the words
have flowed more easily than I imagined. Reading them afterward, now that's the difficult part. Admittedly, this prolonged
act of reflection has come as a blow to my sense of humility.
Looking back, it's quite clear that Maya clouded my capacity for
rational judgment, though knowing what I do now, I must argue
a degree of innocence.

I returned to the loft at eight-thirty with a full belly and
renewed spirits. The light on my answering machine blinked at
me. I pushed the message button.

"It's Henry. You still sound worried. Call me. It's seven."

There was a beep followed by a second message.

"Seven forty-five. Going out for a few drinks. What are you
doing tomorrow? I'll talk to you in the morning."

I called him up and left a message. "Met me at the Modern
tomorrow. Two o'clock in the lobby." I went into the bathroom,
applied the spirit gum remover, and started peeling away the
beard from my face. My heart rate began to speed up. She
won't be there, I assured myself, just accept it. I had already

woven many elaborate alibis as to her whereabouts. Why was I playing this stupid mind game? I wondered.

I called upon my willpower and walked with slow, precise steps toward the front room. The light from her hall chandelier still burned. A spark of hope awakened in me. Back and forth I scanned the unmoving landscape. The bed had not been touched, nor the mirror moved. The now-familiar sting of frustration began to rise. How could she be so cavalier about the electricity bill as to leave the light on all afternoon and night? Then I was shaken by a discovery. The videos were no longer on the television set.

I waited at my perch, poised for her imminent return from the video store. As the hours mounted, my pride dwindled away. How close had I come? I wondered. By midnight I couldn't stand the humiliation any longer. Reluctantly, I conceded that she'd gotten the better of me.

I brought a second red photo album with me to bed—the one with reproductions of Henry's portraits alongside my original photographs—but it didn't give me much in the way of consolation. To date, Henry has completed three of the past residents. Victoria will make four. The album opens with the first sublet photo I ever took of Claire. Next to it is the first painting Henry made of my photos. "Woman by a Window," he titled it. I studied the right-hand corner of his canvas. The building's gray brick façade was easily recognizable. Paula's chapter was packed with telling likenesses of the furnished apartment. Every bedroom portrait contained the long and narrow dracaena leaves draping down and brushing against the four-paned window. In "Woman Thinking," the back of a television set, and in "Feet of Woman," a swash of red carpet gave way to a hardwood floor hallway. All these details started making me nervous. True, any one alone might not have been cause for alarm, but to add them all together? I already knew Maya's eye for detail from the way she studied Degas. My mind was made up. He wouldn't like it, but I was going to have to tell him to postpone the show.

Don't get me wrong. As it has matured, I've come to adore Henry's work. He extracts something from my subjects that photo emulsion simply can't capture. It's difficult for me to describe it with words, but the way he blurs what is in focus in my shots, and the way he puts in focus what was blurry before, allows the viewer to zero in on the crucial details of the scene. He employs an Impressionistic style, but his obsession with framing and focus make his work feel unique. The truth, however, is that it took a lot of effort on my part to help him to find his stride. What seems natural now, the way he brings out the quiet vulnerability of a woman alone with her thoughts, is the result of months of arguments and struggle.

Henry wasn't always such a successful, fast-talking New Yorker. I first encountered him back in the summer of 1991, the third year of subletters, when Laura was my tenant. He worked in a tiny espresso bar on Ninth Avenue called Gossamer. The modern decor of the place was reminiscent of a jumbo jet. Sleek steel tabletops and counters. Silver-glossed sponge-painted walls. Electronic dance music on the stereo. It was a scorching summer, a week straight of temperatures in the nineties, and I had ducked in knowing the café would be well air-conditioned.

Henry sat at a table taking his lunch break. He wore a pair of overalls and a baseball hat turned backward that kept his long hair out of his unshaven face. His sketch pad lay open for everyone to see, a call for attention. At first I thought it an embarrassing display, he was like an actor practicing a monologue on the sidewalk. On top of it all, his technique was flat. Sketches of feet and hands. Basic Drawing 101 exercises. A self-absorbed artist sketching at a café, I remember thinking. The scene verged on

parody, but just as I was about to write him off, something
charmed me. The more I watched, the more I saw a young man
starving for acknowledgment. By sketching on his break, he was
standing up for himself, proving to all those who'd look at his
pad that his life was better than this minimum-wage job.

A healthy-looking young woman wearing a tight white
T-shirt and small turquoise running shorts bounced over to him.
"Gorgeous," she said.

He looked up at her with a cross expression. "Excuse me?"

"They're gorgeous."

He blinked a few times, mumbled a thank-you, and went
right back to work. She remained at his side as he drew, but he
didn't pay her any attention. His restraint amazed me. Clearly, if
he had wanted to, he could have procured a phone number or
signed her up to pose for him. After another few minutes of
being ignored, she turned and left. I made a move over to his
table.

"Do you mind if I have a look as well?" I asked. "I'm
something of a collector." His eyes widened and he pulled out a
chair for me.

"Please. You want some coffee?"

"No thank you. The lemonade will do. You're a student?"

"Yes."

"At the academy, I take it."

"How did you know?"

"Just a guess. The formal style gave you away." I took my
time flipping through them. Naked women, the occasional inan-
imate object—ice skates, vases, wine bottles.

"You think they're too traditional?"

"I didn't say that. Where are you from?"

"Indiana. Right outside Indianapolis, but I've lived here
for four months."

"Four months! What's your name?"

"Henry."

"Well Henry, are you showing at any galleries?"

"There's going to be a group show next month on the twenty-first."

"A show in the summer? Where?"

"Langley Gallery."

"It's a start, I suppose."

"You said you're a collector?"

I stopped at a page where he'd drawn a model in an unusually natural pose. Here his style had changed. The lines flowed much better, and he abandoned the stifling realism of the previous attempts. The girl stood with her arms folded, one hand up near her mouth, as though she were chewing on a fingernail.

"Now *this* is something."

"You like it?"

"The best by far. What happened? What made you do it this way?"

"I don't know. She wasn't really posing. We were wrapping up. I rushed it. Kind of an accident."

"Accident! What do you think of it?"

"I almost like it. I'm not sure."

"Well allow me to be sure. You need more of this, a lot more." Then the idea struck. "Henry, I'd like to buy this sketch."

"But it's not really even done."

"No, I don't want you going back and ruining it. It's perfect as is. What's your price?"

"I don't know, I'd have to think about it."

"Six hundred dollars."

He could not reply.

"Six hundred sounds fair, doesn't it?"

"That, yes. That's fair."

"Come with me to the bank, I'll get you cash."

I took some time to get to know him before introducing him to my secret project. He showed me his studio. An abysmal hole on Rivington Street on the Lower East Side. Hardly any light, no shower, an electric hot plate for cooking beans and soup. Dirty clothes and charcoal sketches covered the floor. This is what I mean about the bohemian fantasy. Perhaps that's why I liked him so much at first, he was like a caricature from the pages of art history, a budding Modigliani, and that allowed me to jump in and play a part as well. My role? Benefactor. First thing, I set him up with a new studio in a building I own in Hell's Kitchen. Twice the space of his old place, and I cut him a deal on the rent so that he'd pay the same amount.

Two or three times a week I'd take him to dinner at some of the city's finest spots. He did his best to look presentable, combing his hair into a ridiculous part, donning an old sport coat and mismatching pants. "Forget it, Henry," I finally told him. "Stop wearing these silly clothes. This is New York. We'll just pretend you're famous, and they'll have no choice but to serve you."

Next, I bought him memberships to the city's museums. His knowledge of contemporary art was atrocious. He was all romance when it came to artists—loved painting from the Renaissance up through Impressionism and not a whole lot else. Our first field trip together found us at the Whitney for a prominent video artist's latest installation. On one wall there were men ass-fucking, on another a crossing guard leading a single-file line of children, and on a third wall, footage of a flock of flamingos. Henry looked flummoxed, practically sickened. "Relax," I told him. "Just try and absorb it. Don't think."

"Why are you doing all this?" he asked suddenly.

"All what?"

"Why are you helping me? The dinners, leading me around. Finding me a better studio."

"Because I see potential, Henry. It is my duty as a patron of the arts to help those with a future."

He paused, and weighed the decay of my words to make sure I was serious. "Thanks."

"You're welcome."

"I mean it. I want you to know up front that I appreciate it." Then he stopped walking and his brow hardened with mistrust. "You're not gay, are you?"

"What?"

"I'm just asking. It's all right if you are, I just don't want to give you the wrong—"

"Henry, please! Is it because of the way I talk? I've heard this before. I swear, if you speak the least bit clearly in this society, people think you're either gay or British. I take it you're not impressed with this room."

"It has nothing to do with the way you talk."

"Well what then?"

"What do you mean when you say potential?"

"I won't be asking you to fuck me later, if that's what you're worried about."

"What?"

"Henry, I look at you and I see a relic from some other time. It's as if you've been hurtled forward a hundred years and plopped down before me. You study at a school that teaches a style nobody cares about anymore—"

"So it's pity. Thanks, but I don't want pity."

"Hold on. I don't mean it as an insult. In fact, it's exactly what I admire. You approach art from a pure aesthetic perspective. That's unique in this day and age. If you'd ask anybody else, they'd tell you that painting is dead. Impressionism? A forgotten fossil. It's like you weren't privy to the latter half of the twentieth century. Conceptual art means nothing to you. And that's your strength, because everything comes back around again, and when it does, you'll be way ahead of the game."

Over the next few weeks he worked on a painting for the group show. I made frequent trips to his studio to check on his progress. He steadfastly held on to his strict representational style despite my prodding to loosen up.

"I only want to help, Henry."

"Maybe you should wait until I ask first."

"How did you get the Langley show anyway?"

"A friend of somebody I went to school with."

I studied the canvas—a woman's vertebrae, from the middle of the back up to the neck. Technically decent, but, like all of his work at that time, utterly devoid of thematic content. "There's something missing here. Style alone isn't going to do it."

"Your opinion."

"Yes, my opinion. Haven't you ever heard of constructive criticism?"

"You talk like you think you know what's right for every single artist. I paint how I paint. It's natural, so stop trying to change it."

"Natural? You were trained to paint like this."

"Well maybe I happen to like it. Maybe I'm happy with how this is turning out. Stop trying to dictate—"

"Now that's not fair. I'm only suggesting you open up. Explore a bit more. Nothing drastic. Believe me, I could more than live on aesthetic beauty alone, but the dealers will want more. The press will want to have something to hang their hats on. They'll want to build you into something important, and that means you've got to come up with a new rub."

"Stop talking and let me get back to work."

On the evening of the opening, his canvas looked oddly anachronistic next to the shock-value assemblage and minimalist found objects that filled the rest of the gallery. "That alone is a victory," I told him. But the fact was that no one paid his piece any attention. "Let's go out and get some food. We'll have some good wine to lift your spirits."

At the restaurant he launched into a tirade. "Bullshit pseudo-intellectuals. Putting a tire in the center of the floor! Big fucking deal, a tire. It's an insult. How do those people get away with such crap? Stuffed animals, sewing garbage bags together. I don't get it."

"I liked the garbage bags," I replied.

"It's just pure . . . What? Laziness. These people can't even draw. How can you be an artist and not know how to draw?" He raised his voice to an unpleasant level. "Pure laziness. It probably took her all of five minutes to do that piece. And what, it's supposed to be some cut-down on fashion, big fucking deal. Big fucking critique."

"Could you please stop with the fucking? You're making the other customers anxious." I winked at the maître d', who looked on nervously.

"Sorry."

"I thought the garbage bags were pretty, but I agree with most of what you're saying. Try not to take it personally. Trends come and go."

After two bottles of a luscious California cabernet and a three-course meal, he quieted down.

"You know, one thing I like about your painting is that it reminds me of a photograph I took the other day."

"I didn't know you were a photographer," he said, and slapped his hand on the table. "All this time and you never tell me you make art."

"I snap off a few now and again, no big story to tell."

"Will you show me sometime?"

"Seriously?"

"Yes, seriously. I'd like to see them."

"I suppose you could, but I'd have to get your word that you won't tell anyone anything about them."

He laughed. "What the hell are you talking about?"

"You can see them, but only if you promise."

"Okay, I promise. Just so long as you haven't murdered anybody."

"Don't worry. Shall we go right now?"

It was mid-August. I was six weeks deep into Laura, and I knew that as it was ten o'clock on a weeknight, she'd be preparing herself for bed.

"This building's amazing," Henry said as he gazed up at the gargoyles and ivy carved into the corners of the façade.

"1902. D. W. Edwards was the architect. Did a lot of the early skyscrapers in Chicago. This is where I grew up."

"Your parents still alive?"

"They live on the bottom four floors, but they spend most of the year in the South of France. Come back for autumn." We got into the elevator. "They gave me the loft apartment as a graduation present. It's a little less cramped than my old room."

"Not bad, but I could never live above my parents."

"Around Christmas it's a bit trying. My mother always knocking on my door with egg nog and sweets. She's a talker, my mother is. Always going on about this or that. 'Pull up your shades, dear. It's sunny out. It's not healthy sitting around in the dark. Not healthy at all. Why don't you get out and take in some fresh air?" He laughed at the haughty tone of my impersonation. "What about your family? Still see them?"

"My younger sister lives on the West Coast. I see my mother once in a while. Don't get along with my father."

"What do they do?"

"My dad was a foreman at a steel mill. When he retired he became a full-time alcoholic. I was fifteen, I think."

"Sorry to hear it. Were you a poor family?"

"We didn't have the money to buy a SoHo town house, that's for sure. We weren't the worst off people in our neighborhood though. My parents had a car and owned the house. I guess we were pretty poor."

"And you still get along with your mother?"

"That's about the right way to say it. We communicate. Phone calls. She tells me she worries about me and I tell her not to worry."

"Sounds familiar. What do they think of your painting?"

"Hate it. They didn't want me moving to New York. Think I'm throwing my life away. Art doesn't make sense in their world."

"I know how you feel. My parents tend to see art as decoration. They like a painting only if it goes with their color scheme."

"Mine it's that they don't get it at all, period. The walls of that house are completely bare. Wood paneling, that's what makes sense to them. Let's not talk about my parents, it just gets me depressed."

Upstairs he gave an appropriately reverent amount of attention to my art collection, even though I knew he didn't care for most of it. "Who's this by?" he asked, inspecting the chrome cylinder mounted on the wall above my kitchen table.

"Charles Hardigan, one of his early pieces."

Henry gave a skeptical hum.

"Too abstract?"

"It's fine." He made his way toward the living room, where he contemplated a Roy Lichtenstein painting. A repeating pattern of red and white pixels surrounding an empty cartoon caption bubble. "Is this an original?"

I could only laugh in response.

"Of course," he said apologetically. Then he arrived at his own drawing. It took him by surprise, mounted and framed and dominating a piece of prime wall space. He stared at it as though he didn't recognize his own hand.

"That one's not so bad," I said. "Got it for a steal."

He was utterly without words, his mouth agape and his eyes glazed over and fixated on the drawing. So grateful he couldn't yet look at me. "I . . ." He searched for the proper thank-you.

"It's all right, Henry. You don't have to say anything." I went into the darkroom and got my black folio of photographs. "Have a seat." I tested his reaction to a few close-ups. They didn't look dissimilar from run-of-the-mill art school figure studies. I handed him the out-of-focus shoulder shot that his painting reminded me of, then one of the small of Laura's back and buttocks as she lay facedown upon the bed. "Very nice," he said.

"Don't feel obliged to give compliments."

"No, I like them. They're very naturalistic."

The third photo marked a change. Laura, naked, standing a few steps away from the window. I had pulled back on the telephoto to reveal the building façade and windowpanes. The larger perspective was laid bare. Henry squinted and picked up the picture for closer inspection. "Incredible!" he exclaimed. "Is she your neighbor?"

I passed him another shot of her getting dressed after a shower. "Lives right across the way."

"Jesus. Is she there now?"

"I don't know. Shall we take a peek?"

"You mean?"

"I mean, shall we see if she's there?"

"Sure. No, wait. She won't see us, will she?"

"No. She thinks this place is abandoned. I boarded up all the windows on that side."

He looked confused but not altogether displeased. "What about your parents?"

"I remove the baffles before they return."

"And then put them back up to spy?"

"That makes it sound so creepy. Come on, it's fine."

"All right. Just for a second." We went to the darkroom and Henry bent down to the eyepiece. "She's there," he gasped.

"Alone?"

"No, there's a man, young man."

"Black hair?"

"Yes."

"Her boyfriend. What are they doing?"

"Talking."

"Sitting on the bed?"

"Now he's standing up. Kissing her. On the mouth, now on the forehead. Picking up his backpack. Wait, leaving the room now. I can't see him anymore."

I checked my watch. "Going to work. A doorman at the Century Bar."

"You know him?"

"Seen him outside the club."

"Aren't you afraid of getting caught?" He stood up and looked at me as though my response would determine the fate of our relationship.

"Well, you strike me as the trustworthy sort, Henry. Am I right?"

"I'm not talking about me. Of course you can trust me. I don't care if you're a Peeping Tom. To each their own. I'm talking about really getting caught." He gestured to the camera. "What if she found out?"

"I've taken the proper precautions."

"But it's totally illegal, right? Invasion of privacy."

"I'm not sure it is illegal. I'm not breaking and entering. She has left the window uncovered. It can't be against the law to look, can it?"

"But it's a setup. It's fraud. You'd be in deep shit if you ever got caught."

"You're probably right, but I won't. Tell me, Henry, you're an artist. Don't you find it necessary to take risks now and again? Doesn't your work ever depend on it?"

"Sure, I guess. It's just that breaking the law—"

"The law! Henry, this is a victimless offense if ever there was one. I'm not out to get the poor girl. She'll never be the wiser."

"So what will you do with the pictures?"

"Nothing. You're the only person I've ever showed them to. Up until now the piece was for an audience of one, me. I love that idea, private-access art. Nothing for sale. No critics to please. It's a pure expression, no compromises."

"But you decided to show me."

"True. An unexpected detour."

He let out a bemused laugh and lowered his eye back to the camera lens.

"I've seen things here, Henry. Real things. A real side of this woman's life. How she puts both her stockings and shoes on before her skirt. How she clamps her left hand over her eyes when she masturbates. We lead a whole other life when we're confident no one is watching us. That's why models are no good. Call it spying if you want, but this experiment might be the only way to get at that life. It's not just a matter of being a Peeping Tom. I'm not doing this for my jollies. Sure, I enjoy looking at pretty women, that's part of it, but more than that, it's about capturing something that's normally out of reach. Don't ask me to explain every detail. I don't want to understand every single motivation. Art was never meant to be spelled out. There has to be a sense of mystery involved, even for the artist. No, scratch that, especially for the artist."

"I still don't get why you chose to show me."

I walked into the living room and came back carrying Henry's framed drawing. "Because of this, Henry. I felt something when I saw this. I imagined a possibility. I think your art could really benefit from what I'm doing here."

He looked at me suspiciously. "How?"

"Come look at some more pictures," I said.

The next day he visited again, this time bringing a sketch pad along. He'd look at her for hours at a time, then retreat to my kitchen and try to re-create her from memory. For a week it went on like this. Often I left him there while I went out to run errands. Those first drawings caused him a lot of duress. He never quite pinned down the sensation of looking at an unsuspecting subject. Finally I suggested that he work directly from my photographs.

"I can't do that," he said. "It's cheating."

"Your imagination is getting in the way. You're clouding over the thrill of the voyeurism."

"What do you mean?"

"This isn't a girl posing for an art class, Henry. Don't try to turn her into a model. This is real. That's what I keep trying to get through to you. She's real, living in real space. Don't shy away from that fact, it's the whole point. You're drawing like you're afraid someone's going to find out your secret. The highest art requires truth. Focus on the details that make this different from the artificial act of sketching a studio model. My advice? Take a couple of prints back to your studio. I won't tell anyone, if that's what you're worried about. After all, this is now a partnership. I trusted you and you've got to trust me."

"But you're sure you don't mind? They are your pictures. I can't just copy them, it's—what's the word I'm thinking of?"

"Plagiarism?"

"It's plagiarism."

"Whatever works, Henry. It's not like I'm going to try to sue you. Besides, everything nowadays is plagiarized. Haven't you heard? We've run out of new ideas. It's all retread at this point. Besides which, I'm not convinced different mediums are capable of plagiarizing one another. Now go home and start painting. I'd like to have some time alone with Laura if you don't mind."

"I don't like the sound of it. Not from your pictures. I can't."

I had to laugh at his flimsy ethical protestations.

"What's so funny?" he demanded.

"Tell me, in art school, didn't they ever make you copy a painting?"

"Sure, we did Goya, the Saturn Devouring one, a technique exercise."

"Right, of course you did. Probably did you a hell of a lot of good, am I right?" He didn't answer. "So why not do a few from my photos? It's called process, Henry, and if it happens to lead you in a positive direction, well then what in God's name is so troubling? I'm giving you my permission, after all."

He thought for a moment, then went back to shaking his head. "Sorry."

"All right, all right. Let's try something else." I stood up, went to the living room bookshelf, and returned with a volume of Degas's paintings. "Another assignment. I want to commission you to paint me a reproduction."

"I'm not interested in doing knockoffs—"

"I'll pay you eight hundred dollars," I said, and opened the book to my personal favorite. "Here's the painting I want."

" 'The Rape,' " he said.

"The what?"

" 'The Rape,' we studied it in one of my seminars."

"Well your teacher didn't get the title right, for one. It's called 'Interior.' "

"No it isn't. 'The Rape,' I'm sure. I like this one, I remember it specifically."

"Henry, the title is right here on the page."

"That's probably an old book. Maybe that's what it used to be called, but we discussed it in my class for a long time. You see the way her clothes are on the ground like they've been ripped off?"

"Don't go twisting it, Henry. There's a story behind this painting. *Therésè Raquin,* the novel by Zola. You did discuss that, didn't you?"

"We did, actually, but that's just one interpretation. The book probably influenced the picture, but there's no proof that Degas was doing it straight from it. Most everybody these days thinks it's about a rape. See the man in the corner? He just did it to her, then got dressed and is about to take off. Look, she's crying."

"Amazing that we're talking about the same painting. He is not about to leave, and furthermore, she isn't crying, at least not in that way. They are thinking, Henry. They're locked in thought. I'll lend you the novel if you like, that'll prove it. You know this whole way of seeing history amazes me. There's a term for it. It's a movement. Historical revisionism, right?"

"I don't know."

"That someone can just come along years after the artist

has done his work and slap on a new title and story line. It's despicable, really."

"I'm just going on what I learned."

"I don't mean you specifically. Your school. Your instructors."

"But it is a fair interpretation, from what I see anyway." He picked up the book. "Not everyone who sees this in a museum is going to know about the novel. To them it is a rape. Who's to say they're wrong?"

"I am, Henry. They're wrong. Period. Sure, fine, let them believe what they want. I'm not saying that art always has to be about coming up with correct answers, but by the same token, we must not go too far the other way and say that because two people have different interpretations, correct answers don't exist in the world. Sometimes there are right answers. The title 'The Rape' is not the right answer."

"Don't get so defensive."

"I am not getting defensive."

"Okay, fine."

"Forget the title. We'll drop the subject. If you want to delude yourself, go ahead. The question remains, will you paint this for me or not? I want it to scale, thirty-one by forty-four inches. Can you do it?"

"Eight hundred?"

"Eight hundred."

"Tell me again. Why?"

"It'll go with the rug in the rental apartment."

"Seriously."

"I like the tension in it. And I think it might help."

"Help what?"

"Your vain obsession with creating something from scratch."

He took a few moments with the picture, and I sensed him plotting his attack. Where he'd begin on his own canvas, how he'd duplicate the color and warm light. That meeting was just over two years ago. Three months later he finished the reproduction. We were both surprised by the quality of the result. "Ready for your next assignment?" I asked.

"You're not my teacher, you know."

"Only kidding, Henry. But I would like you to have a crack at this." I handed him an eight by ten of Laura wrapped in a white towel, lifting a black coffee mug to her lips. "You can take liberties with this one if you like. Same deal as before. Eight hundred."

He took the picture and stood over his version of "Interior," comparing the two.

"There's a similar quality, don't you think? Not a very subtle influence, really. Peeking at someone's private life," I said. "That's why I had you do Degas."

"Listen, let's forget the money. The deal is that you agree to let me work from your photographs, but the paintings belong to me. You've given me enough money already. No more commissions."

"Fantastic."

"And we don't tell other people, right?"

"Right."

"I mean we don't tell anybody. As far as the world is concerned, I came up with the idea for this in my head."

"Your secret's safe with me. I'll protect you and you'll protect me." I went to the cupboard and removed a bottle of scotch. "A partnership. I knew you'd come around."

●

Maya's second day. The photo album lay open on my chest when I awoke in the morning. I took a shower, placed Strauss on the stereo, and dressed in character. In the bathroom I carefully applied the beard. All the while I resisted the lure of the camera lens. I had a point to prove. I wasn't going to waste another day circling around the apartment. I went downstairs, got the *Times* from the doorstep, and sat at the kitchen table flipping through the Arts section. I made an espresso and downed it in one gulp. Calculated movements. Self-control. You're strong, I murmured as I picked up my briefcase and headed for the door. No, I couldn't do it. The pull of the darkroom was too great. I turned and darted in for a check.

No change. Nothing. Videos gone, the bed still made up, light in the hall still burning away. I bit down on my bottom lip until I tasted blood. The beginnings of madness, I thought.

My first stop was the public library. I found the Shoichi Noma Reading Room empty except for a middle-aged male Chinese librarian. Save for his short asthmatic breaths and the soft ruffling of the pages of his book, the room was quiet. Clearly, I was the day's first customer—no books out, and the chairs were tightly aligned against the expectant tables. Strangely, a great impatient stirring in my head caused me to forgo my usual routine of contemplating the compositional impact of each position around the room. Unlike past days, when such a choice might have given me great pleasure, I rushed to the far side of the table to my left and set my briefcase down in the same spot I had sat ten days before. Nor did I bother to look up and admire the outcome of my rash actions. These were not conscious decisions. I simply wasn't paying any attention, and that is perhaps the most unusual aspect of it all.

Instead, I went directly to the shelf to retrieve *Death in Banaras* only to find it missing. I browsed the titles back and forth to make sure I wasn't overlooking it. The main branch is not a lending library, so the book should not have left the building. Perhaps someone had taken it to another room. Disappointed, I selected two other volumes: *A Popular Dictionary of Hinduism* and *Banaras and the Buddha*.

I picked up the book on Banaras. The reading was dense and in an English I found difficult to penetrate. A tale of the Buddha renouncing the decadent, sheltered life of a prince and setting out into the world to travel the road of asceticism, or so the anonymously written introduction informed me. But harsh abstinence doesn't prove to his liking either, so he sits down by a river, meditates, and comes up with something called "the middle path." The story's moral, I gathered, that one should avoid extremes and find balance.

Everything in moderation. A repulsive conclusion if you ask me. Art demands risks, not moderation. Artists have always reserved the right to use extreme tactics, to live off balance. Without those willing to test the edge there would be no progress in the world, no earth-shattering novels, paintings, or skyscrapers. I thought back to something my father once told me: "First and foremost, religion is about order. About keeping people in their place." Well put, Father. And art is about destabilizing that order. I snapped the book shut and pushed it aside.

The word "bindi" was my next query, and I found it in *A*

Popular Dictionary of Hinduism with a slight deviation in spelling—the final *i* replaced by the letter *u.* I experienced a hot
flash when I read the definition on page 67.

> bindu: dot, drop, globule; in philosophy: the meta-
> physical point out of time and space where the absolute
> and the phenomenal meet, which is experienced by
> some types of Sanadhi (meditation); the sacred mark
> made on the forehead, symbolizing the third eye (the
> eye of wisdom); in the Tantras: semen; Siva's semen, the
> essence of life and the symbol of the nectar of immortal-
> ity; the symbol of Brahman, the essence of all reality.

". . . metaphysical point out of time and space . . ."
Hadn't J. P. Parry's book given a similar bit about Banaras? I
also seemed to recall a mention of Siva, the god of destruction.
Siva's semen upon Maya's forehead? Perverse. I reread the passage a couple of times but still couldn't get past the part about
the absolute and phenomenal. How could those two concepts
exist on the same plane? From the little I knew of Judeo-
Christian philosophy, I thought that a person experienced either
one or the other. The absolute a kind of heaven, or root cause,
and the phenomenal the product of the absolute, or the state of
the world as we know it through our senses. When we are alive
we dwell in the phenomenal. After death the absolute—or so
say those with faith. The notion of an all-seeing eye appealed to
me. With it one might sneak a glance into the great beyond
without the mess of dying.

Back to the shelves and another book. *The Dhammapada,*
a sacred text of Buddhist aphorisms. This I learned from Purnell
Duxburry, an Oxford scholar from fifty years ago, in the first
paragraph of his simply worded introduction. But by then I was
tired and only browsing, flipping my way past whole chunks.

Still, under the heading "Chapter 5, The Fool," I stumbled on a passage that struck me as sufficiently interesting to write down.

If a traveler does not meet with one who is better, or his equal, let him firmly keep to his solitary journey; there is no companionship with a fool.

Like the very best horoscope or fortune-cookie message, the universality of the words allowed my imagination to run off on multiple interpretations. Perhaps Maya was the traveler and I the fool. What did the journey mean in metaphoric terms? Was it my experiment? Where did Henry fit into this equation?

My thoughts strayed back to the bindi. Almost an hour had passed. I took off my glasses and rubbed my eyes. Soon I'd have to leave for the museum. Just as I was about to search for another book, a loud guttural scream echoed down the hallway, followed by a tremendous crash. The librarian and I looked at each other for a moment before jumping up and running out into the hall. Not twenty feet down the corridor lay an old man. He had fallen forward and toppled over a wooden chair. His belongings were scattered everywhere. Ratty paperbacks, halves of old sandwiches, and soiled newspapers. He kept eerily still. The librarian and I rushed to his aid. The stench from his tattered clothes was overpowering. Others soon arrived and helped us flip him over onto his back. His long gray beard glistened with saliva and mucus. His yellow, glazed-over eyes stared up at the ceiling.

"Call 911," a young woman ordered.

"Does anyone know CPR?"

The Chinese librarian went to work on the man's chest. But he soon informed us that it was no use. No breathing. A crowd circled around us, buzzing with questions.

The paramedics arrived and lifted the lifeless body onto a

stretcher. "God he smells," one of them said. "Looks like a heart attack." They were gone in a matter of seconds, leaving the straggling onlookers with no single focal point. Many shook their heads and turned away. I remained there by the stairs, looking down into the lobby and all the people oblivious to what had transpired.

Man in poor health climbs a flight of stairs, suffers a heart attack, and dies. It must happen hundreds of times a day, but why so close to me? It was as if I were meant to see it. No, I wouldn't let paranoia get the better of me. This was not the work of some larger system of order, not the absolute paying a visit. I ran my fingers through my false beard and discovered that the corner at my right sideburn had come unstuck. It dropped down like a loose flap of skin. How long had it been that way? The spirit gum was in my briefcase. Then I realized that I'd left my glasses back on the table. I gave a quick look around to make sure no one had noticed my appearance and rushed back to the small reading room, holding my hand to the side of my face as if I had a toothache.

●

I arrived at the Modern just after two. The lobby was full of high school tourists who had just gotten off a bus from God knows where. Clustered in one group, the boys all wore baseball caps, the brims curled so as to obstruct a clear view of their eyes. The young women, in their own pack a few feet away, chose floppy, beachlike headwear that also obscured the face. What were these teenagers hiding? I wondered. Each one sported a "Hello, my name is . . ." sticker on his or her baggy flannel shirt, and without fail, every one of them was in blue jeans that looked five or six sizes too big. The entryway echoed with their laughter and shouting.

I caught sight of Henry slouching in the corner, a scowl on his face. He wore a brown leather jacket and old porkpie hat.

"Where's your name tag?" I asked as I approached.

"What? Oh, it's you. I almost forgot the beard-and-glasses routine."

"Let's go in. Beat the hordes."

"They're from Indiana."

"Your people! How do you know?"

"I overheard one of their teachers."

"And I thought *you* dressed like a slob."

"That's the style these days. It's everywhere."

"So you're saying even a backwater state like Indiana is on

the cutting edge? This globalization thing has gotten out of hand."

We flashed our membership cards and proceeded to the special exhibit. I feel completely comforted by the Museum of Modern Art. It's like visiting the home of a fond relative, familiar smells and all. Even though I have come to appreciate the aesthetic world outside museum walls, the synthetic environment still whets my appetite for great works, even if it only rarely delivers. For me, the mere prospect of looking at art elicits a sense of optimism. I see only potential. Not so for Henry, whose trepidation toward today's show was more than evident, judging from his expression. Despite my tutelage, three years in New York have hardened his outlook, brought him into the cynical fold, as it were.

"Preparing yourself for the worst?" I asked.

"Did I say anything? I haven't said a word."

"Your face says it all."

He put on a contrived smile. "Trying to have an open mind, okay?"

"Henry, the strangest thing happened just before I came here. I'm still trying to sort it out."

"What? What happened?"

"This is going to sound crazy. I was at the public library and a man collapsed and died not twenty yards from where I was working."

"What did he die of?"

"A heart attack. At least that seemed to be the consensus."

He shrugged. "People die."

"Thank you, Henry, I'm well aware of that. The disturbing part was that I had just been reading about something called a bindi."

"A what?"

"It's that red dot Hindu women wear on the forehead. You

see, what's strange, scary really, is that I had just finished a passage that defined the dot as the essence of life, as the very symbol of mortality, when bang, there's this awful scream and a man dies right before my eyes. Now maybe you don't find that odd. Maybe I shouldn't either, coincidence and all that."

"Why were you studying this dot in the first place?"

"Maya, Henry. Maya Vanasi, who is the new tenant, wears the bindi."

"She's Indian?"

"She is."

"So now you're branching off into multiculturalism, is that it?"

"Very clever, Henry."

"I still don't see the connection."

"Perhaps I'm projecting. Is that what you're telling me? These things happen."

"Sure they do. All the time. Say you're walking down the street humming a song, then you go into a store and the same song is playing on the radio. Or you think of a word or a movie, and then the person you're talking to says it out loud."

"So, you believe in some sort of psychic link?"

"I'm just saying coincidences happen."

"Do you know anything about the Buddha?"

"I thought you said she was a Hindu."

"She is. At least I assume she is. But she's from the same town as the Buddha."

"Ah-ha. Now I get it. You've decided that they're related or something, is that it?"

"All right, Henry. That will do."

"Forget about the dead man. It doesn't *mean* anything. Tell me about last night. I'm dying to know." We entered the corridor containing the first section of Cecilia Muñoz's installation entitled "Dead Cells." The floor was painted red and overlaid with pale yellow crescent shapes that looked like clipped fingernails. Human hair of all shades coated every square inch of wall space. The contrast of rich colors gave the room an inviting, tactile intimacy.

A young couple stood beside us, holding hands. The woman took a quick look around for security guards and then reached out and patted a brunette patch with her pale white hand. I stopped walking and admired her inquisitive strokes. Yes, she was right, the hair wanted to be touched. Having crossed the sacred line that keeps us from truly interacting with art, this brave young girl would come away from the show with a better understanding of the piece than most. No sooner did that thought cross my mind than her curmudgeon of a boyfriend jerked her arm away and whispered, "Vandal! You should be arrested."

The lovers laughed and moved on. I went to the spot she'd stood and touched the silky stuff for myself. "Beautiful, don't you think, Henry? All this hair. I wonder where Ms. Muñoz found it. A barbershop, no doubt. It's real all right."

Henry stood a few feet away, unwilling to come any closer. "I don't get your thing for hair."

"What do you mean?"

He gestured to his chin.

"Right, the beard. You see, this is why I drag you to these shows, you show me things about myself I've overlooked. You're absolutely right. I like that link. Maybe she's saying that art itself is a kind of disguise."

"Quit with the philosophy and get to what happened last night. We'll talk about whatever the hell this is later."

"You know you've really grown quite close-minded."

"No, I've always been this way."

"Have you? I thought it was that before you simply didn't know very much about conceptual art, not that you didn't care for it."

"I have *never* liked this kind of stuff, and I happen to know plenty about it, for your information."

"But you never sounded so superior. When did that happen? Have I created a monster?"

"Just like you to try to take the credit."

"Or the blame, as the case may be. Well, I still have hope for you. It's an acquired taste."

He closed his eyes in disgust. "The story! What happened? Is everything going well?"

"Not exactly. I haven't actually seen her yet. I think she might still be staying at her hotel."

"No pictures?"

"Not yet."

"Should I come over yet?"

"Choose the day. Only I'm telling you, there hasn't been much to look at."

"What's she like?"

"You'll be pleased."

"Dark hair?"

"A beauty. Not like the others, and I mean it this time. I was looking at the photos last night. This is going to be unique. All new poses. Maybe it's because she's from another culture, but even the way she stands is different."

"I'll believe it when I see her."

"That's another thing I need to talk to you about, the paintings. Bad news I'm afraid. It seems she knows Dianne Handsforth quite well. She said Dianne had taken her out to her place in the Hamptons."

"What are you saying?"

"Calm down."

"No, what are you saying? Are you telling me that just because your new tenant knows Dianne Handsforth that you want me to cancel my show?"

"Henry—"

"No, don't even try and start with that. This is an important show. It's all worked out, I can't just pull out now."

"Well what if you just postponed it?"

"Postpone! Are you serious? What are you trying to do, kill my career?"

"Henry, there's no need to take this personally. And you don't have to raise your voice."

"The show stays."

"Okay."

"No, I mean it, fuck you. The show stays. Do you hear me? The show goes up."

People started spreading out away from us in that hair-coated room. Even when he's quiet, Henry's an imposing presence, but it's truly frightening to watch him lose his temper.

"Okay. You win. The show stays. Now would you do me a favor and lower your voice?"

"The paintings aren't a problem. Do you hear me? Why don't you trust me for a change? If I tell you the paintings aren't a problem, then they aren't a problem."

"I trust you, Henry."

"Do you? You're so full of shit."

"For crying out loud, Henry, put yourself in my shoes. It's not my fault that Maya happens to know the gallery owner. Please excuse me for being a wee bit cautious."

"The show goes up."

"Fine." I knew he'd react this way, but I had planted my seed. Later, when he'd cooled off, I'd be able to see the paintings in question. By this time the tour group had caught up with us, and their clatter sent us into the next room, where we were greeted by an oversized bronze cast of a single turd resting on a wooden pedestal.

"Brilliant!" Henry exclaimed. "Can we go now?"

W e lunched at an Asian-French fusion restaurant called Vong. Sea bass in a delicate broth, succulent chicken satay, a bottle of Montrachet. For dessert, a sampling of tropical sorbets. Henry was uncharacteristically silent through the meal. Feeling guilty, I surmised, that he was enjoying my generosity so soon after his museum outburst. It's always this way. He gets hot, throws his tantrums, and comes back around.

"I'm sorry," he said after I paid the check.

I put up with him for my own selfish reasons. It's gratifying to know I'm the one most responsible for the steady improvement of his artwork. Influence. As far as I can tell, that's the best part about being a benefactor or parent. "Apology accepted, Henry. You've no choice but to act the part of the passionate artist. I know how important this show could be."

"If you don't feel comfortable after you see the stuff, we'll try to work something out."

"Thank you."

"You're not angry at me, are you?"

"Stop. Of course not. Tell you what, how about we go and see if a certain bird has come back to her nest?"

"Sounds good."

We hailed a cab. In the backseat I looked up at the driver's identification card. I was taken aback to realize that I recognized him. "Weren't you the man who took me to the Old Memorial just the other day?"

"Where?"

"The Old Memorial. One Hundred and Twenty-fifth Street, near the Apollo. It's a little hotel."

"Now I remember. Yes. Not today going there, are you?"

"Downtown," I said, and gave my address.

"What were you doing up in Harlem?" Henry asked.

"Looking for Maya."

"Is finding her that hard?"

"You don't know the half of it."

The driver looked back at me quite often along the ride. Squinting, examining, studying my face. It was terribly disconcerting until I realized the reason. He had remembered our trip to Harlem, perhaps even my voice, but not my face because of the beard and glasses. It amused me to watch him puzzle over my appearance, and I let out a little laugh when he furrowed his brow.

"What's funny?" Henry asked.

"Tell you later."

We got out. The taxi slowly rolled away from the curb and didn't speed away until we were at my doorstep. I stood on the stoop and followed the cab until I couldn't see it any longer.

"What? What now?"

"I don't know exactly. This has been a most unusual day. Scratch that, a most unusual string of days."

"Why? Because you got the same cabdriver two times?"

"Not just that."

"You're not still stuck on that old man dying, are you?"

"Maybe a little."

"When did you become so superstitious?"

"Come on. Let's go up."

"You're not kidding. You're serious."

"I can't give you a satisfactory explanation, Henry, but there's been a pattern of irregularities ever since I met Maya."

"Maybe you're in love."

I laughed. What a refreshing thought. "Maybe, Henry."

"Well I can't wait to see the beauty that's causing you such trouble."

"Don't get your hopes up. She's probably not going to be there."

Love. No, I can't speak about love with very much authority. Throughout my lifelong career as a bachelor, I've had numerous first dates, but only a dozen or so follow-ups. Money will get you that far. Into an expensive, trendy restaurant. Theater tickets, a private tour of a museum, perhaps even a late-night invite up to an apartment. Occasionally sex, depending on my date's level of self-esteem. It rarely reaches that point, though, because at the first hint of insincerity or charity, I'll put an end to the night. While wealth affords me lots of initial opportunities, my money is also the thing that ruins it for me in the end. I'm too proud to be used or pitied.

Age has helped my odds a bit. A certain category of aspiring younger women opened up to me once I hit thirty. College girls, easily wooed by an older sensibility. Ripened bodies, underdeveloped minds. And yet here again, I'm my own worst foe. I demand too much—mental maturity *and* striking physical beauty. I'm the first to admit that I'm going for a caliber of woman who'd never have me. Darwinism gone awry, my aspirations have led me to a dating pool beyond my reach. So I go along channeling whatever energy it is one saves for love into my projects. Sad and true, but I have no regrets. None I want to put down on paper anyway.

In the darkroom I obliged Henry with the first look through the camera. "Hot damn!" he exclaimed. "Not bad at all."

"What!" I pushed him out of the way.

"Hey, wait your turn."

My face flushed with blood as I caught my first frame of her. She stood by the bedroom window, pouring water from the porcelain pitcher into the dracaena. My reflexes kicked in. I checked the camera's setting and clicked off one, two, three pictures.

"Jesus," Henry said, "what the hell's she doing? Taking off her shirt?"

"Just standing there, watering the plants."

"You were right, she's a looker."

She wore a white button-down blouse and a brown skirt whose hemline I couldn't see, as she was standing so close to the window. A new outfit. Had she unpacked? She took special care with her task. Watering, waiting, then watering again. Five, six, seven photos. Her hair was down. From my angle I couldn't tell if she was wearing the bindi.

Henry nudged me in the ribs. "Don't go hogging the damn thing. Let others have a chance."

Reluctantly, I let him take the eyepiece.

"Yes sir," he said, "a fine-looking woman."

"Why? What's she doing?"

"Nothing. Calm down."

For the next twenty minutes we took turns observing her. I snapped off a whole roll of thirty-six-exposure film. She watched television for a short while, then went into the kitchen out of our view. "Probably making a sandwich," Henry said.

Finally, she came back out and walked over to admire Henry's reproduction of "Interior." I was happy for him and let him have the camera. An artist rarely, if ever, has the opportunity to spy another person's genuine admiration of their work. Gone are the false compliments, the obligatory praise. Henry stood transfixed at the sight of her absorption in his and Degas's painting. "I think I may be falling in love with her too," he said.

"Tsk-tsk, Henry. You know the rules. No contact with the tenants."

"She loves my work. How can I not love a woman who loves my work?" But then his demeanor sharply turned. "Wait!" he yelled. "Wait, wait, wait!"

"Let me see. Out of the way."

"What does she think she's doing?"

"Move, Henry."

"She's taking the painting down."

"Goddammit, get out of my way." I pushed against him, but he didn't budge.

"What the fuck is wrong with this woman?"

"If you don't move out of the way this second you'll never set foot in this apartment again."

"Christ!" he exclaimed. "I can't believe this. I am not in love. For the official record, I am most definitely not in love with her." He slapped at the camera and stomped away.

"Henry! Have some respect for the equipment." I repositioned the tripod and witnessed the cause of his rage. She had moved a chair in front of the fireplace, flipped the painting around, and set it on the mantel so that it faced the wall.

●

Not long after Henry had gone, Maya stepped out. It occurred to me that they might pass each other on the street, and I wondered if Henry would have the willpower to resist confronting her. No use trying to explain that Maya's reaction to the painting was more a compliment than an insult. I removed the film from my camera and shut the darkroom door. A single red bulb bathed the room in diffuse warm light. Despite Henry's histrionics, I felt overjoyed by the turn of events. At long last I'd have a product to show for all my efforts, perhaps not even the most interesting shots, but a product nonetheless.

I assembled the various accoutrements required to process the negatives, shut off the light, and threaded the edges of the film into the developing tank. Then I added the proper chemical mixture, set the timer, and waited. This stage in the routine always sends me back to the summer my father taught me photography. For my tenth birthday he bought me a thirty-five-millimeter camera and simple darkroom kit. To my mother's dismay, we commandeered the guest bathroom. Enlarger, chemical baths, clothesline to hang the prints.

On our first picture-taking outing we went to Times Square, which, back in 1973, wasn't exactly the tourist-friendly destination it's trying to be today. What's incredible about New

York is that with the possible exception of the late 1970s, since its inception, the quality of life has continually improved. We got out of the cab at Forty-first Street and Eighth Avenue, smack-dab in the middle of the bums, prostitutes, and saloons. "We'll make our way to the Square," my father instructed. "Take your time, and stay close to me."

"What am I supposed to do?" I asked.

"Look at the people closely. Try to find something interesting about them."

"What do you mean?"

"Don't worry so much. If you see someone you like the look of, take a picture."

"Do I have to ask them first?"

"Only if they see you and look like they'd mind. Just you watch, most people won't even notice."

We got home an hour or so later and shut ourselves off in the makeshift darkroom. He read each step out loud from the manual, refreshing his own memory and teaching me in the process. My mother knocked on the door. "What is that smell?"

"The chemicals, dear."

"Is it always going to be so strong? It's not right to have to live in such a state. What will our guests say about these dreadful odors wafting about?"

To a child's eyes, the magic of photo emulsion, of dipping the prints into the bath, is something akin to a miracle. "Here it comes," my father said. "I told you it would."

I shouted out in awe as the first gray pixels materialized on the floating photographic paper.

Father's pictures went for the grit of Times Square. Street people mostly, as well as a few cops and a hooker. They were filled with passion, gestures, conflict. In short, narrative. They told the story of the down-and-out. Drunken bums holding out soiled paper cups for change, a merchant marine passed out on the sidewalk. I suppose these subjects fascinated him for how different they were from his own posh existence. All in all, it was a very liberal-minded photo essay.

Mine, on the other hand, was much more ambiguous. Men in business suits, as stiff as Secret Service agents, standing in static poses at the crosswalk. A waiter at a restaurant writing an order down on a notepad. A newspaper boy's profile. Cabs waiting for the traffic signal to change. "Good first effort," my father offered. I'm sure he dismissed the shots as naive, but to this day I'm proud of them. They seem almost iconographic. The raw materials of a ten-year-old's mind.

I stayed with photography through high school, where I grew convinced that the only pictures worth taking were candids. I despised posed shots. Loathed photographers like Raymond Alladon and Fran Lesser. All those big-shot movie stars! To my young, immature way of thinking, their portraits were nothing more than glorified public relations shots, pure vanity. Energy, that's what I yearned for, to catch a life in a raw, unfiltered state.

I hit the streets every day after class let out, Leica hidden just inside my jacket, and staked out different corners of the city. Pretending to tie my shoe, I crouched down and surveyed the passing crowd. Then I'd unzip my coat, set the focus and depth of field, and wait for interesting-looking people to pass by. Mr. Penn liked what he saw. "Yes! Get them with their guard down," he said in his authoritative German accent. "A fly on the wall, that's what you are. A true fly on the wall!" Since then, I've come to realize that all of public life is a pose, that in a place like New York there's really no such thing as a candid picture. When you step outside, you're on display. Ask any anthropologist. The very act of observation changes the behavior of a subject.

The same holds true for the animal kingdom, as I discov-

ered back at the end of my senior year of high school. My
parents and I took a spring break trip to Kenya's Rift Valley. Our
guide pressed the point again and again that our best chance of
getting an action shot would come if we took the animals by
surprise. We'd spy their natural state for only a split second. As
soon as they sensed our presence, chances were they wouldn't
continue to hunt or mate.

Touring the countryside by open-air Jeep, I grew over-
heated and nauseated. I'd eaten some sort of deerlike creature
for dinner the night before, and it was starting to let me know I
shouldn't have. As luck would have it, we rounded a bend and
happened upon a cheetah streaking across the plain after a
gazelle. In my haste to get a good shot, I dropped my camera.
The back popped open a crack when it hit the ground. "For
God sake!" cried my mother. "Don't tell me you ruined the
whole morning's worth of film."

My father jumped to my defense. "Harriet, stop yelling at
the boy. I'm sure it was an accident."

"The film's all right," I assured her. "Nothing to get worried about." When I returned home to the darkroom, I found
out otherwise. Come to think of it, that was the last roll of film I
developed before starting Columbia. I graduated high school a
few weeks later and Mother packed up the equipment without
even asking. The message was clear, in college I'd have no time
for such a trivial hobby.

After my five-year layoff from photography, I upgraded the
darkroom equipment and refined my technique so that now I
can compensate for poor lighting conditions, even a lack of
focus. Therefore, I can say with certainty that in preparing
Maya's roll, there wasn't one step out of the ordinary save the
extra amount of care I administered to insure the highest quality. How, then, to explain? An hour and ten minutes later, when
I cut and placed the six plastic strips upon my light table?

Overexposed, blurred negatives. Faint shadows. I printed up a couple of shots just to make sure. There were beginnings of images—the border of the window, and what looked like her shoulder—but they were so burned out with streaks of light that more often than not I wasn't even sure what I was looking at. But I knew the effect quite well. These were the very same results I'd seen in the Kenyan safari photos. The pictures were a total loss. I crumpled the negatives and threw them in the trash.

What about Henry's swipe at my camera? If the latch had come undone, the film could have been exposed to enough light to ruin the roll. But I soon discovered another detail that made it hard to hold him fully responsible. The date on the exterior of the film carton had expired over two months before. I was stunned at my error, for if nothing else, I consider myself a careful man.

Maybe the camera was to blame. To make sure, I fetched another film carton from the refrigerator—date of expiration good for another year and a half. Maya wasn't home, but I clicked off the whole roll anyway to test the camera. The building façade, empty window, the living room, and that damn hall light still burning. I plucked out the film and followed each step in the developing process with painstaking precision. An hour and ten minutes later I had my answer. The camera was not the culprit.

I printed up all the exposures and studied the photos that evening in between glances through the camera's eye. Though she'd interacted with the environment—returning the videos, flipping the painting—Maya still hadn't moved a single item into her new home. I grew quite angry. Even if she hadn't checked out of the Old Memorial, why would anyone in her right mind choose to stay there when she had such a luxurious alternative? My face began to itch from the dried-up spirit gum, and it surprised me to find that I was still wearing the beard.

T he morning came with no news to report. I called Henry. "The pictures didn't come out."

"What do you mean?" he asked. "They were out of focus?"

"Washed out. Bad film perhaps. What do you think?"

"What do you mean what do I think?"

"Couldn't have been when you hit the camera?"

"I barely touched it."

"Not possible that the back opened up?"

"Christ! Listen to you. You think I wouldn't tell you if I'd exposed your film?"

"Just asking, Henry."

"Jesus Christ!"

"Don't get pissy. Listen, when can I come over?"

"Whenever you want."

"One o'clock?"

Silence.

"Don't be mad, Henry. I believe you. The film was bad, that's all. It's just a little frustrating. She hasn't been in the apartment all night again."

"She'll show up. At least you know she's watering the plants."

"See you at one, Henry."

I pulled out Victoria's album from the bookshelf and sat on

the couch. The pictures are laid out in chronological order, from the Polaroid taken at her interview to the eight-by-tens of her last hours in the apartment. Victoria. "Named," she was quick to point out, "after the romantic novel by Knut Hamsun, not the queen."

Her charm lay in her innocence. Poised to be poisoned, I thought when I met her. There were other applicants that summer who surpassed her in beauty but none who matched her naiveté.

"I'm from western Pennsylvania," she announced at the interview.

"Where exactly?"

"You haven't heard of it, trust me. Fishkill, it's near Carlisle."

"You're right, I haven't heard of it. A pretty place?"

"The prettiest. We live right on the river, and there are mountains just behind us. Well, not mountains, big hills."

"What brings you to New York?"

"A friend of my friend's dad got me a summer job at a fashion magazine."

"Which one?"

"*A-Line.*"

"Very impressive."

"You've heard of it? We don't get it out in Fishkill. That shows you how small we are. I've only ever seen it a couple of times."

"It's one of the better. Much more exclusive than the supermarket rags."

She was beaming, proud that she'd done the right thing. Such low aspirations!

"And do you know many people in the city?"

"I have a cousin, Simon. He's a great guy. Really cool. He

works, well, not works, he owns a big nightclub here. It's called
Cul de Sac."

"Really?"

"You know it? My God, that's great. Have you been
there?"

"Once, briefly." It was a cocaine den. Loud industrial music and decor to match. Young people looking for dark spaces
and thrills, acting out with their shabby style of dress and rude
behavior. Fascinating on a sociological level, pathetic on any
other. "I take it you haven't been there yet?"

"I've been trying to get ahold of him. I think he might be
out of town."

Two weeks into her stay, the cousin appeared at the apartment with an entourage in tow. I knew it must have been him
by the way he carried himself as if he were of some importance.
She reached out to hug him, but he hardly responded. The crew
of tagalongs, two women and one man, barged into the living
room and turned on the television. Victoria gave her cousin a
tour of the apartment, and they stayed in the bedroom to talk.

I clicked off pictures wildly, making sure to get a close-up
of each one of them just in case they tried to steal anything. The
two women went into the bathroom together and came out
wiping their noses. The other young man deposited himself in
the armchair and fell into a television trance. Rather abruptly
her cousin stood up and led his friends away, leaving Victoria
behind in the foyer. I wondered if they hadn't had an argument,
for she didn't move away from the door for several minutes.

The very next night, however, she spent two hours preparing herself in front of the full-length mirror. She tried on no less
than four different dresses. I got several shots of each one before she decided on a hopelessly out-of-step shortsleeve number. She combed her chestnut hair this way and that, put it up

into a bun, and finally let it fall naturally. The sound of the doorbell caught her off guard, and she made a last-second dash for shoes. Simon's crew had returned, minus one of the women. Including Victoria, it was now two boys and two girls. She'd been set up with the fellow who so fancied my television. At this point I ran out of film and had to reload. By the time I lowered my eye back to the lens, they had gone.

One o'clock, not home. Two-fifteen, still not home. Two thirty-four, the front door opened and she and her date stumbled through the entryway, drunk beyond any doubt. In the living room he moved on her in ruthless fashion. She pushed him away, and he landed in the recliner. He jumped back up and was at it again. Her body tensed with fear. I could tell that she was yelling at him to stop. It was playing out all too predictably, so I reached for the darkroom phone and dialed.

The first ring slowed his progress. She managed to break free and run into the kitchen.

"Hello," she panted.

I disguised my voice. "It's your neighbor. I heard yelling. Do you need the police."

"Who is it?" I heard the man yell.

"Yes, please, send the police."

"The police!" the man shouted.

"They'll be there soon." I hung up and returned to the window. He was already on his way out the door. She bolted it behind him and backed up into the kitchen, out of sight. All was still for a long, long time. At last she wandered into the hall. It is this series of pictures that are my favorite. The long march from hallway to bed, a dazzling mixture of shame and relief on her face. I went with a quick aperture setting to get a low light, grainy texture that perfectly emphasized the mood. She collapsed on the bed and lay on her stomach for close to an hour. I thought about calling to ask if I should cancel the call to the police but decided to spare her the humiliation.

Why did I intervene in Victoria's drama? I trace the answer back to the television nature specials I watched as a boy. When I was around eight or nine years old I developed a near-hysterical hatred of cameramen who filmed these programs. Their footage revolted yet enthralled me. I never missed a show, nor did I ever fail to end up in tears. In particular, I remember a sequence in which a mother wolf's teeth gnashed into the downy fur of a rabbit's belly. A second camera unit revealed that the camouflaged filmmakers had gotten within a mere fifteen feet of the action. "How can they just sit there and not help the rabbit?" I cried. "They can stop the wolf. Why don't they run up and scare it away?"

"There's no use fighting it, son," my father assured me. "Nature has its own laws. Nothing to do with sympathy per se. Besides, if the cameraman wasn't there, the wolf would still kill the rabbit. They're just recording what already exists."

"Isn't sympathy part of nature too?"

My poor father. He let his hardcover book come to rest on his lap and took a few contemplative puffs from his pipe. "Not always," he said. "No, not even most of the time."

As a young boy I naturally identified with the rabbit and demanded intervention. Like most children, I couldn't come to grips with the brutality of existence. Throughout adolescence, I entered another phase. Realism started to dominate my thoughts. I came to see the world as my father did. Nature had its plan, no use fighting against it.

It may make me sound naive, but it wasn't until I became an adult that I learned how nature specials are made. The numerous tricks directors employ to arrive at the organic-looking finished product. Stock footage, studio sound effects, phony locations, even substitute animal actors. Really, the result is no different from the fantasia of a Hollywood movie. The amount of fabrication came as a revelation, and I can see now how that discovery influenced the development of my apartment project. In fact, it was right around the same time that I tempered my restrictions on realism.

As I've said, I came to desire more control over my tenants' daily lives, but that wasn't why I stopped the boy from assaulting Victoria. To me it was a question of subject matter. I didn't fill the apartment to watch a woman get raped. I wanted a more subtle piece than that, and so did Degas when he painted "Interior," despite what some upstart art critic might believe.

Over the next days and weeks, Victoria sank into a terrible way—an existence dreary to watch and beautiful to photograph. She stopped going out at night. Upon returning home from work she'd change into her pajamas, pour herself a large glass of milk, and plop down in front of the television set. Two or three hours of unfocused staring at the screen. "The look in her eyes reminds me of a character in a Hopper painting," Henry said during one of his frequent visits. "I feel like I should go over there or something."

"Why?"

"To cheer her up. It's awful to watch her sitting there."

"You can't very well just knock on her door. 'Hi, I've been spying on you for the past few weeks and I couldn't help notice that your life isn't working out so splendidly.' "

He stood up from the camera and walked over to a row of eight-by-tens that were hanging on the line to dry. "I could pretend I was a deliveryman or the gas guy. Start up a conversation, take her to dinner."

"Rules are rules, Henry. No contact with the tenants."

He touched his fingers to the surface of one of the prints—

a close-up of her tear-swollen face. "She's really a fantastic subject."

"Exactly. Why ruin a good thing?"

"That's cold."

"Have you started painting her yet?"

"No, but I can tell already. I can work with her."

"How's Laura coming along?"

"Better. I think you'll agree."

"Keep up it, Henry. We'll make an artist out of you yet."

In the days that followed, Victoria took to ordering out. She loved Chinese, and only rarely stooped to pizza. Because the living room recliner faces the window, I was able to take my time with the pictures, and came to anticipate her slightest movement. Lots of heavy sighs. Once or twice she lapsed back into tears, an echo, I guessed, from the earlier trauma.

Her telephone didn't ring much, or if it did, she didn't bother answering it. On weekends she'd sit and read the Travel section of the *Times*. Stories of far-off places. New York was just as distant to her as Cairo or Venice. That she rode the Number 4 subway line through the heart of the city each working day was incidental. I doubt if she looked up at the passengers around her. My apartment sheltered her from all of it. Neither her cousin nor his friend ever showed up again. In fact, the only other visitors were her parents, who spent a weekend in the city right at the end of her stay. Before they left they helped her pack up her big suitcase and took it back home in their red Volvo station wagon.

The last three days, Wednesday through Friday, she didn't leave the apartment at all. This struck me as odd considering she had gone to work the previous two. With no greater evidence than her body language, I gathered that there wouldn't be a future for her in magazines. No, her New York foray had been a mistake. She now resigned herself to smaller things.

It took her a while to answer the buzzer when I rang on Saturday morning. "Welcome back," she said. "How was your trip?"

"Rained nearly the whole time. Hardly got a single shot."

"That's terrible."

"Very frustrating. What can you do? Here." I unzipped my duffel bag and removed a green-and-red wool blanket. "A present from the rain forest."

"Jefferson! Thank you so much. It's beautiful." She looked close to tears. "I love it. You didn't have to get me a gift."

"For taking such good care of the apartment. Tell me about your stay. Did you enjoy New York?"

"Very much."

"Manage to hook up with your cousin?"

"Yes. I went and saw him at his nightclub. It's huge."

"It is that. And the job? Am I looking at the city's next great fashion editor?"

She managed a laugh. "No, I don't think so."

"Didn't take to the rat race?"

"It was a good experience. I'd come back someday. There are other things I want to do first, but someday."

"Sounds like a plan."

H enry's Hell's Kitchen studio is on Forty-fifth Street between Tenth and Eleventh. Much to his chagrin and my financial delight, it's a changing neighborhood. The city council, with its own stroke of historical revisionism, passed a resolution to officially re-recognize the district as Clinton. Fewer and fewer prostitutes walk the streets, and most of the heroin pushers have pushed on elsewhere. The rents are on the rise, and I won't be surprised if he decides to find a new space in another, less affluent part of town. He's attracted to grime. "I don't know how you can live in SoHo. All those rich people pretending they're bohemian, all those obnoxious stores. Everything's so fucking overpriced."

When I arrived I found all the works in question propped up against the walls of his studio. I set my umbrella down by the door and walked to the center of the room. Their beauty nearly paralyzed me, and for a few moments I forgot the reason I'd come to inspect them. Proportion has become Henry's strong suit. With sharp technical accuracy, he captures the smallest details of form. Fingers, noses, torso dimensions, the tilt of a neck. Granted, the translation of my photos onto canvas is no simple feat, but without the pictures as a starting point I doubt he'd have improved so much and so fast. The growth in his work since Laura was clear and gratifying to see.

Standing before the paintings, I grew flush with a renewed sense of Victoria's supple skin. He'd conquered the sense of volume, the weight of her arms as she stretched them above her head. The grace of her movements. I took a few minutes with each one, looking from across the room, then at point-blank range.

The magnificent trick of a representational painting is that the more you try to focus on it, the more it is reduced to mechanical gestures—paint, brush strokes on canvas. I'm talking about something very simple, and, perhaps with the noted exception of Pointillism, often ignored. Upon first glance you see the thing, the painting's subject, but then, the closer you study it, the more you lose it amid the technique. Then, just when you think the subject might dissolve for good, your eye clicks back and you find it again. In the best paintings this transition is fluid and never hinders your enjoyment of the piece. You experience form and content on even terms. With the Victoria series, Henry had merged the two brilliantly.

But the longer I looked, the more my resolve solidified. This show had to be stopped. "You know that what I'm about to say has nothing to do with the quality of your work—"

"Stop. Stop right there. Stop talking, you've hardly been here two minutes. Give it some time."

I walked over to a canvas and pointed. "What is this, Henry?"

"That happens to be the best thing I've probably ever done."

"I'm asking you to describe what I'm pointing at."

"Looks to be a painting hanging above a mantel. Many people hang paintings above their mantels. It's a standard in home decorating, if I'm not mistaken."

At the next canvas I pointed again. "And this?"

"Let me see." He crossed his arms and squinted. "From

where I'm standing, that appears to be a woman looking into a full-length mirror."

"We can stop with the games."

"That's a good one. Stop with the games. You? You telling me to stop with the games is just about the funniest thing I've ever—"

"Henry."

"You waltz in here and you pick out the two paintings of the whole bunch. The two that—"

"Don't play stupid, Henry. Please don't. Every one of these has a hint, a clue."

"What's the clue in this one then?" He picked up one of Victoria standing at the window in her pajamas.

"Put it together with the rest. The fact that she can stand so close to the window. The proximity of the window to her body."

"It's a woman and a reflective pane of glass. There is nothing here, nothing, that puts you at risk." He began circling the room and ran his hands through his greasy hair.

I knew I'd better back off or this wasn't going to end well. "All right. Maybe there are some that are less obvious than others."

"So you're telling me you want to sort through them one by one, is that it? You want me to let you have total veto power? This one's in, and this one's out. I'm sorry. You can forget it."

"I thought that's why we set this meeting up in the first place."

"Maybe you should just get out."

"Henry, it's me you're talking to. The person who's been supporting you. You'd still be working in that crappy little café if I hadn't come along, not to mention the studio."

"I never asked you to buy my paintings."

"That's right. But when somebody goes out of his way and

treats you as well as I have, don't you think you owe them an ounce or two of courtesy?"

"Owe you? I don't owe you anything. You want to buy a painting, fine. You don't, that's fine too. This isn't one of your complicated real estate deals. I paint how I paint. Let me do what I do. I knew this arrangement was going to be a problem. I knew it. The answer is no. I'm not going to let you censor my work. You don't own these, and you don't control me. Get the fuck out. Now!"

"For crying out loud, would you please calm down? I'm not trying to censor your work."

"That's sure what it sounds like. When you talk about this one's in and that one's out."

"What I'm trying to do is keep us from getting thrown in jail."

"Oh please."

"Try to think clearly for a second. What if Maya did recognize the apartment? Have you asked yourself that? She recognizes the television, or the mantel, or the windowpane, or the floors, or the mirror, and she goes home and she looks out the window. She thinks, 'I wonder where the person who painted those pictures was looking from?' Then she takes the time to really study the boarded-up façade of the place across the street—"

"Okay—"

"She sees a circle cut into the wood that appears to be reflecting back a small glimmer of light. Then she remembers my instructions about keeping the windows uncovered for the plants—"

"Okay. Shut up already. I get your point."

"Well it's about time."

We were silent for a while. I looked over the rest of the paintings. He was right. Far and away, they were his best. Each one captured the emotion just so. In Victoria he had found a perfect subject. A forlorn quality that spoke to him, that inspired something higher. The undeniable truth of the images could not have been evoked by a model, nor could it have been conjured in the world of the imagination. No, only the voyeur had access to a performance so lacking in self-consciousness. "I love them, Henry. I mean it. They're beautiful. You've come so far, it's astonishing."

"Don't ruin this opportunity for me."

"I won't. Reason shall prevail. For you and me both."

Two interminable days followed in which, as one might guess at this stage, Maya failed to make an appearance. Through it all, the bulb in the hall fixture burned a hole in my retina and an ulcerous wound in my stomach. My bewilderment mutated into a bubbling rage at the callous creature who had bound me to such a futile routine of watching without reward. I sank further into a rut of repetition. The order on the stereo went Strauss-Stravinsky-Beethoven and repeat. Pacing the apartment, I applied the beard, took it off, applied it again. I ordered sushi for lunch and then for dinner. Eating, pacing, watching. Eating, pacing, watching.

That damn bulb glowed like an ember in my brain. I began fantasizing about sneaking over and shutting it off. Only then, I told myself, would I find peace of mind. Bound up the stairs, open the door with my spare set of keys, a few short steps across the foyer to the switch, and back out. Thirty seconds, no more. But what if I failed to hear her footsteps behind me? What look on her face to find me there? And I knew myself better than to believe I could enter the apartment without giving a quick inspection. To the drawer in the bedroom to see if the bookmark had been moved, then the hall closet. No, I'd be trapped for sure. I'd just have to suffer through the steady stream of light and pray the bulb burned out.

As for Maya's whereabouts, I narrowed down the possibilities to two—the Handsforth beach house in the Hamptons or the squalor known as the Old Memorial. Perhaps I'd employ Henry for a little detective work with his Ms. Handsforth, but first I'd make another pass by One Hundred and Twenty-fifth Street.

●

Again, a gloomy day. According to a pie chart on the front page of the *Times,* we'd had more rain this summer than in the previous four combined. Thunder rattled the sky as I stepped into the cab. My driver was a balding black man who didn't hesitate when I gave the address of the hotel. A baseball game blared from the radio, and every so often he moaned his disapproval at the success of the opposing team. A wind stirred the trees in Central Park, and people picked up their strides at the promise of a downpour.

"I'll only be a minute," I told the driver as we pulled up to the curb.

"You've got to pay first. Thirteen fifty."

"But I'm coming right back. Keep the meter running."

"You've got to pay me now."

"All right. Fine. But you'll wait here for me? I'll just be a second, really."

The man nodded in reply.

The door to the Old Memorial was ajar, and I entered without ringing the bell. The smoke was thicker than before, and the character of its smell had changed from cigarettes to that of cheap cigars. The same out-of-date calendar hung on the wall, with its buxom pinup girl. I wondered how many years would pass before they'd notice it. Behind the Plexiglas shield an old man sat as motionless as a wax figurine. Smoke wafted up from a cigar at his side. The sound of the same monotonous ball game echoed from a radio somewhere. It gave me an eerie feeling to hear that identical sound track—the slow cadence of the announcer's voice, the intermittent crowd noise and static. It made the room feel as though it had been waiting for my arrival.

"Hello," I said. The man gave no response. "Excuse me, I was hoping you might help me." Was he deaf? "Excuse me." Perhaps the volume of the radio was too loud. "Hello!" I shouted.

"Hold on," a woman's voice yelled back. She entered the vestibule from a door behind the old man. I recognized her from before, the one with the wig. "What can I do for you?"

"Perhaps you remember me. I was here a week or so ago. I was, well, I still am looking for an acquaintance of mine. I know that she stayed here, and there's a distinct possibility that she's still staying—"

"Name."

"Yes, Maya Vanasi. You remember, I came here—"

"Spell it."

"V-a-n-a-s-i, but, you see, we've been through this."

"When did she check in?"

"Look, we've gone through this before. I just need to know if she's still here or if you've seen her. Maybe your friend here has seen her."

"What does she look like?"

"Dark skin. Not black. Darker than mine. She's Indian. Sometimes she wears a dot on her forehead."

"I remember you. You went and grew a beard."

"That's right. Now, about—"

"Looks good. I like it."

"Thank you. Thanks."

"You're still searching, huh?"

"Have you seen her?"

She leaned down and spoke into the old man's ear. He nodded and pointed to the center of his forehead. Then he leaned forward, flipped to a page in the registry, and tapped his finger on a name.

"Checked out this morning," the woman said.

"That's wonderful news. He's seen her then, the one with the dot? He's positive?"

"He's seen her all right. Says she left not half an hour ago."

"Great news. Thank you very much for your help. Good day to you both." I turned to leave. Finally, I was making sense of it all.

"Mister," the woman called just as I was opening the door. "Only one thing. You got the name all wrong. Not Maya Vanasi."

"What do you mean?"

"Checked in here under the name Thompson. That's why I didn't find her here the first time."

"Thompson?" I headed back to the desk.

"What it says here. Mara Thompson. London, England."

"Wait. Hold on. Mara, M-a-r-a? From London?"

"M-a-r-a T-h-o-m-p-s-o-n. Want me to spell London for you?"

"Do you mind if I have a look?"

She held the book up to the scratched surface of the Plexiglas, and I read the words just as she had recited them. The first name sounded so familiar. Where had I heard it? Or was it simply that it was so close to Maya? This had to be her. The handwriting and signature on the page looked like I imagined it should—feminine and steady—but I'd never seen Maya's script before, so there was no way to verify it one way or the other. I flashed back to her comment about not knowing if Henry's reproduction of "Interior" was authentic. Christ! If I had only gotten her to fill out an application. The radio hit a patch of static and cut off my train of thought. "This was signed by the woman with the red dot, he's certain?"

"Certain as certain can be."

"And she spoke with a British accent?"

The woman bent down and asked the old man, who gave several deep nods. Then I noticed a crucial detail. Mara Thompson registered on Friday, June 25, the day after I interviewed Maya. But Maya had made it sound as if she'd already been sleeping at the hotel. She knew, for example, that there wasn't a phone in the room.

"You need to see this anymore?" the woman asked.

"No, thanks."

"Think it's her?"

"Could be. Can you ask him just one more thing?"

"Sure."

"How old would he say the woman was?"

Hearing the question, the man hunched his shoulders and shook his head. "He's not very good with telling age."

"Approximately. Young? Old?"

She spoke my words to the man, but the reply was the same. "Sorry. Guess when you get as old as he is, everybody just seems young to you. Probably didn't really pay much attention to it. Don't matter how old you are as long as you pay in cash."

I let out a sigh. "Okay. Thanks anyway." I stepped outside, but the cab had driven off. The temperature had plummeted, and right on cue the first large drops of rain started to fall. "What next?" I shouted.

●

With no cabs to be found, there wasn't much choice but to resort to public transportation. I ran three long blocks through the pouring rain to the elevated subway tracks. The overwhelming sensory immediacy of the train car helped distract me from my troubles. In fact, it lifted my spirits to remember how orderly and efficient the subway can be. The riders around me showed great regard for one another, spreading out to let a panhandler by, never failing to offer their seat to an elderly woman. Incredibly civilized. The row of passengers across the car—two rotund black women with bulging, recycled Macy's bags, and three black boys of varying ages, each wearing a different color baseball hat and elaborate space-age basketball shoes—seemed to take turns glancing at the advertisements above my head. Their facial expressions were solemn and passive, the same as is common in elevators. People crowded into a small space, doing their best to be invisible.

I, too, looked up at the row of ads and found a poem by Thomas Hardy, "A Young Man's Epigram on Existence." Four lines which I set about memorizing.

A senseless school, where we must give
Our lives that we may learn to live!

A dolt is he who memorizes
Lessons that leave no time for prizes.

I'm not the greatest fan of poetry, but the simple insight of
these words made sense. We must indulge in life's prizes, I
thought, like reading poems on public transportation.

My only complaint was the ridiculously cold temperature
of the subway car. With those air-conditioning bills, it's no wonder the transit authority runs in the red. The fact that my blue
jeans and shortsleeve shirt were soaked through didn't help. I
clasped my arms close to my chest and held the beard to my
face with my right hand, but as advertised, the spirit gum
proved water resistant. I couldn't say the same for my tennis
shoes.

I suppose the poem and the foreign atmosphere of the
train cleared my mind just enough, for just as we reached Forty-
second Street, it came to me. I stood up knowing where I'd seen
the name Mara. I pushed my way through the crowd and stuck
my foot out just in time. The angry doors clamped around my
soggy shoe, and a man behind me muttered, "Come on. You're
holding us up." The doors reluctantly parted and I darted out.

After sloshing through three more blocks of hard-driving
rain, I entered the library and the Shoichi Noma Reading
Room. All but four of the twenty or so chairs were taken, and
the patrons had distributed themselves so that an even balance
presided between the room's left and right halves. There were
too many people to look at, and I was in too great a hurry for a
long aesthetic calculation on how my seat choice would influence the room's spatial dynamic. I chose the chair closest to the
Indian shelves and picked out the mustard-colored cover of the
Dhammapada from the third shelf from the top.

The woman next to me—white, late forties, academic type

with bifocals, an enormous stack of books and a laptop com-
puter—gave me a cross look as small puddles of rainwater gathered beneath my dripping elbows and pant legs. "Excuse me,
madam, may I trouble you for the use of one of your pencils and
a piece of paper?" I asked, and leaned toward her. She quickly
ripped off a sheet and pushed it in my direction so that I'd stop
my advance.

I turned to the first chapter. It didn't take long to find the
name. It rose up from the page in several passages:

> He who lives looking for pleasures only, his senses
> uncontrolled, immoderate in his food, idle and weak,
> Mara (the tempter) will certainly overthrow him, as the
> wind throws down a weak tree.

And

> He who lives without looking for pleasures, his
> senses well controlled, moderate in his food, faithful and
> strong, him Mara will certainly not overthrow, any more
> than the wind throws down a rocky mountain.

Then later, in Chapter Seven

> One's own self conquered is better than all the
> other people; not even a god, a Gandharva, not Mara,
> could change into defeat the victory of a man who has
> vanquished himself, and always lives under restraint.

I scribbled away, transcribing these and dozens of other
references, but none of them ultimately gave me any greater
context to understand who Mara was or where she came from. I
returned to the introduction, which I'd hardly scratched on my

previous visit. This time I took it slowly and read the whole ten pages, wherein Purnell Duxburry explained that the name I'd found at the Old Memorial also belonged to the Hindu god of lust and sin. Mr. Duxburry warmly referred to Mara as "The Tempter," "The Destroyer," and "The Evil One." This naughty girl had tried, and failed, to seduce Buddha himself, hence all the talk of overthrowing and vanquishing. It was all a bit much for me to absorb, and seemed only to present more disparate threads that would lead me away from my own drama, but I trudged onward and ended up reading nearly two thirds of the book just to make sure I didn't miss any crucial part. Around four, my powers of concentration reached their limit. Too many thoughts had been let loose in my small brain for one afternoon.

Back out onto the drenched streets, where, with what felt like the first stroke of good luck all day, I managed to capture a taxi. The warm seclusion of the cab helped calm me down. The fogged-over windows shielded me from any further visual provocation. Mara, Maya. Mara, Maya. Thoughts of gods and fake names and coincidences and traps. What could I believe? Where did the reality of it all begin? What strange scenario was this that I happened upon?

Back at my front door, my cold, shriveled hands shook as I put the key to the lock, and I let out a sneeze. In a clearer state of mind I would have changed out of my clothes first thing. Instead, I went right to the camera. Nothing. No changes. "Where are you, Mara Thompson!" I yelled.

Crazy scenarios played through my mind. Perhaps Maya had used the pseudonym to throw someone off her trail, but who? Her parents? Her uncle in Manchester? A vengeful lover? But she was so calm at the interview. No, this wasn't a woman running from anything. Why else use a false name? Espionage? I remembered in our first meeting how she couldn't define the purpose of her stay in New York. It was as if she'd know when she found it. This didn't exactly sound like secret agent material. Maybe she'd been at the hotel for a few days before the twenty-fifth, but hadn't actually checked in. Too many maybes. I was a scientist without enough data to construct a sound hypothesis.

Another sneeze. I called Henry to put him on the trail of Dianne Handsforth. His machine picked up. "Call me, Henry. It's important."

I drew a bath and recalled the way Maya had measured the tub. "Partial to measurements," she'd said. What good were measurements if she never used them? It dawned on me then that what I considered a string of frustrating oddities might in actuality be Maya's normal pattern of behavior, one I would have to reconcile myself to. That if I were to accurately measure her, I'd have to throw out my preconceptions and start thinking in different terms. Did the secret to deciphering this pattern lay within the words I had read in *Death in Banaras*? Maybe Maya, like the entire ancient city, stood outside space and time, on a parallel plane of existence. I was grasping at straws. Whatever that new and mystical way of interpreting her was, I didn't know it yet.

The scalding water brought the blood to the surface of my skin as I sank down inch by inch into the tub. Of all the previous tenants, it was Paula who loved to bathe. How different her stay was from Maya's! Paula's Western mind made perfect sense to me. She was all I could have hoped for when I conceived the experiment—the foil I always envisioned. I often wonder what happened to her.

●

P aula Evander. Hair, the lighter side of brown. Squinted when she smiled. She was tall, assertive, trim. Pretty at first glance but not quite beautiful. Hers was a beauty that grew on you. First off, I was taken with her confidence and wit. She was the curious one, up for whatever excitement life put in her path.

"What about music?" she asked during her interview.

"I gather you mean what about loud music. You enjoy playing it at high volumes?"

"Not so loud. I'm a waitress. Work nights. When I come home, it helps me settle down."

"Any particular kind of music?"

"All kinds. Something soft at night."

"Classical?"

"Sometimes."

"What composers do you like?"

"There's a piece by Beethoven that I can't seem to stop listening to. The Kreutzer sonata. Am I saying that word right?"

"You certainly are."

"It's just the first part that I like. The first fifteen minutes."

"Andagio sostenuto—presto. Fascinating story. The piece really wasn't written for Rodolphe Kreutzer at all."

"Who was it written for?"

"One George Augustus Bridgetower."

"Who's he?"

"A violinist. It seems he and Beethoven shared a romantic interest in the same young woman. Messy business. Bridgetower got the girl. Consequently, Kreutzer, a far inferior violinist, got the dedication."

"Poor Ludwig," she sighed.

"Would you like another chocolate?"

"Thanks." She reached into the bowl a second time. "You seem to know a lot about classical music."

"When I was a very young boy, six or seven, I'd stand in front of the mirror holding a pair of chopsticks like two conductor's batons. I'd wave the things around in the air listening to whole symphonies. I memorized Beethoven's Fifth from start to finish. Got pretty good at making up my own signals."

"When I was six I listened to ABBA and Air Supply."

"Don't know them."

"You're not missing much. Elevator music."

"May I ask where you work?"

"Just finished training at a place called Callas down on West Broadway."

"It's pronounced *Cal*las, after that ghastly opera singer. Very chic place. Popular with the paparazzi."

"I've heard stars go there."

"You like stars, do you?"

"As long as they tip."

"You're not an actress?"

"No. I'm saving for an around-the-world plane ticket. Then I'll go back to school. Psychology."

"Travel the world, then come home and try to figure out what you were chasing."

"Think I'll stick to other people's problems. More fun that way."

"You like helping people?"

"My family tells me I'm good at diagnosing people's problems."

"I'll need to take your picture. Do you mind?"

"Not at all. I don't have chocolate all over my face, do I?"

Three days later I dined at Callas. Well, dined is a gross exaggeration. The Caesar salad, overdressed. The tuna, overseared. The crème brûlée, not properly burnt. The serving of food was simply a pretense by which all these showy people showed themselves off. Customer eyed customer, hostess flirted with manager, waitress leered at bartender, and every possible combination of the above. I very much doubt if either the rubbernecking staff or clientele would have noticed if the linguine alla vongole was laced with cockroaches. At least, I thought, they'd got the name of the place right.

Without question the selling point that kept this culinary atrocity in business was—I use the past tense because as of this past January it closed down—the ineluctably ripe smell of fame. One corner boasted a supermodel, the next a film producer. In the banquette sat a grizzled rock-and-roller from the 1970s. Lots of leather outfits, vests, and square-toed shoes. Men wearing glasses with small round wire frames. I suppose they thought the spectacles made them look more intellectual. The women showed as much flesh as the law permitted. They sat cross-legged and tugged at the bottoms of their skirts at regular intervals, no doubt conscious of the fact that in the act of tugging they were drawing more attention to themselves.

The crowd on this evening was of mixed race. Black, white, Asian, Hispanic. They chattered at full volume while loud electronic music thumped away. Flipping her long blond hair to one side, then the other, the undeniably beautiful hostess strutted around the tables as though she owned the place. When she whisked by, all eyes were drawn to her. Men sneaked glances.

Women scrutinized her as though she were a topographic map.

"Is everything all right with your dinner?" she asked me even though I'd just finished my dessert.

"Tell me about your accent. Is it Swedish?"

"Norwegian. Excuse me, there's someone at the door. Enjoy your dinner."

I watched her walk back to the hostess stand. To my delight, the person who had arrived was none other than Paula. I waved, caught her eye, and she came right over.

"Here looking for stars?" she asked.

"Thought I'd give the place another chance."

"Are you alone?"

"Just me."

"I don't like eating alone in restaurants."

"Neither do I. Join me, won't you?"

She sat across from me. "Came in to get my schedule. Are you all packed? Getting excited to leave?"

"Most excited. How about you? Ready to move in?"

"Most ready. I think my friend is pretty sick of having me in her living room."

The hostess came to our table and handed Paula a small slip of paper. "Four shifts next week, Monday through Thursday."

"Jefferson, this is Christina."

"We've just met," I said.

"I think I hear the phone ringing," Paula said.

Christina rushed away. "Pretty girl."

"That's why they hired her."

"You sound like you don't like her much."

"Is what she is."

"And what's that?"

"You want the dirt, huh?"

"If you want to tell it."

Paula leaned forward and lowered her voice. "She's a gold digger. Somebody told me the only reason she got the position is because she's dating the owner. He feeds her a steady diet of cocaine and clothes. I give them about another six months."

"That long?"

We laughed. "You're right, make it three." I loved the cynical look in her eye as she inspected the crowd around us. A blond trollop wearing a floral-print halter top got her most derisive stare.

"Not a bad spot for people-watching."

"Not bad at all," she said.

"All of them so primped and posed."

"They're here to be seen. Check out the one in the purple dress. Trashy!"

"Not the most elegant look."

"How long do you think it took her to put on all that makeup?"

"Hours no doubt. I'm always curious what these people are like when there's no one around to watch them. Do you suppose they ever forget themselves? Do they ever drop the affect? Now that I would like to see."

"I don't think the one in the purple is alone much."

"Good point." I nodded to one of the waiters who was wearing black pants and a tight black T-shirt that showed off his healthy build. "What do you make of him?"

"Lawrence." She paused and followed him with her eyes. "The only straight guy who works here."

"Attractive, no?"

"Sure. Haven't worked with him much."

"So you've yet to complete a full psychological profile?"

She returned my smile. "Give me time."

Paula moved in four days later. I followed the steps of my

recipe one by one, and in no time was enjoying the view from
the telephoto lens. Against my instructions, she was already at
work excavating the closet. She took her time unpacking the
stack of blankets, croquet set, and canister of posters, setting
each item in the hallway in a row so that she'd remember in
what order to replace them. When she uncovered the nine-by-
twelve-inch manila envelope on top of the metal box, she didn't
hesitate. She unfastened the clasps and removed the copy of
Celebrity Skin magazine. There was no mistaking the smile on
her face as she flipped through the pictures of movie stars
caught exposing their breasts to the sun of Saint-Tropez or
Monte Carlo. The paparazzi's relationship with celebrities has
long fascinated me. It's a perfect symbiosis. The bigger the star,
the harder it is to get the photo, and yet the more photos there
are in print, the bigger the star.

Paula soon tired of the magazine and slipped it back in the
envelope. On to the metal box. She weighed it in her hands like
a Christmas present and gave it a gentle shake before taking it
over to the bed. Next she fetched a hairpin from her rucksack
and attempted to pick the lock. "Such wonderful nerve!" I exclaimed. I must have snapped twenty shots on that scene alone.
She gave up after a couple of unsuccessful minutes of jimmying
and twisting, and put the box back in the closet.

The videos occupied her for the next few hours. I believe
she first tried Andrei Tarkofsky's apocalyptic, oblique film *The
Sacrifice*, for she got only a few minutes deep before she ejected
it. The second selection, *Corporal Punishment,* is one of the
more brutal S&M titles I've ever seen. No actual sex, but lots of
slapping, whipping, and nipple torture. I'm not a big porno fan.
It's the intensity of this particular film that interests me. Hard to
find anything that still has shock value these days.

She sat in the armchair for the entire hour and nine minutes of the feature, never taking her eyes from the screen. No outward signs of disgust, she even broke a smile for a moment. Other than Paula, only Laura had bothered with the films, and she had ejected them both after thirty seconds or so and returned them to the store. After *Corporal Punishment* was through, Paula gave Tarkofsky another chance, fast-forwarding her way through his slowly shifting landscapes.

I included *The Sacrifice* in my program for its extraordinary camera movement. The film opens in a wide open field. We see a father and a son standing next to a young tree. They appear more or less the same distance from the camera as the rental apartment is to my own home with the naked eye. Over the course of the next ten minutes, Tarkofsky inches us closer to his characters. The space between viewer and subject slowly collapses until we are delivered into the intimacy of their lives. His restraint is breathtaking. I find this first sequence one of the most patient and inspiring in the history of moving pictures, as well as an apt metaphor for my own relationship with my tenants.

Paula didn't seem interested in decoding the film's unspoken message. She shut off the television and went back to her search. She must have been disappointed that the rest of the apartment didn't turn out to be as fruitful. All, that is, with the exception of finding *My Secret Life*. I could almost hear her doing the mental calculations. One porno magazine, one video, one book, and whatever was in the box. This final tally did not a psychopath make, yet she'd certainly seen enough to wonder about the mental state of her invisible host.

Her investigation of the apartment ended at three. She removed her shirt and jeans, revealing mismatching underwear—black bra and white cotton panties. Next she went into the bathroom and returned drying her face with a towel. She picked up *My Secret Life* and crawled underneath the covers. In a matter of minutes the book had come to rest and she drifted off to sleep. What strange dreams must have flooded her mind.

She kept late hours. Her nightly routine consisted of returning home from work at four-fifteen A.M., a glass of red wine, a bath, and a few chapters of *My Secret Life*. I rose at eleven, just a little before her so as to catch her dressing ritual. She owned an extensive wardrobe and tried on several outfits each morning—short skirts, blouses, medium-length sun frocks, even a black cocktail dress—before deciding on the old standby; jeans and a T-shirt. She rarely left the apartment wearing makeup, but always tested a few different lipstick shades. It was as if she were preparing for some other life just around the corner.

She took to renting movies in the early afternoons. Of what sort I can only guess. Perhaps an X-rated feature or two. At five she left for Callas.

This regimen lasted just over a week. Then, on a Sunday morning at four forty-five, she arrived home with straight waiter Lawrence on her arm. She opened a bottle of red wine and they sat on the living room carpet. The sexual tension followed a soft crescendo. She drew circles in the rug with her index finger, while he inched ever closer. Finally, she took the decisive step, leaning forward and kissing him. They embraced and started rolling on the rug. Suddenly, she jumped up and ran to the kitchen. Lawrence looked confused, then saw the spilled glass of wine. Paula returned with a handful of paper towels and a box of iodized salt. She attended to the stain while Lawrence scratched the back of his head and checked his fly.

Lawrence got down next to her, but clearly wasn't worrying about whether or not the salt would absorb all the wine. He ran his hand along her back and shoulders, and before long, she succumbed. On their way to the bedroom she clicked off the lights and the stage went black. My show was over for the night. In the weak light of dawn I returned to the eyepiece. Lawrence had gone. He hadn't stayed longer than a couple of hours. Paula stood naked by the full-length mirror, drying her hair with a towel. She took a long time to stare at herself, but not the way one looks at pimples or a waistline. It seemed she was fascinated by her own image—like she might be seeing herself for the first time.

The next night Lawrence was back. This time they left the lights on during sex, and I snapped off a solid roll and a half of film. Their lovemaking was neither here nor there. They struck all the standard positions and never strayed from the predictability of the bed. He played the more dominant role. Paula looked subdued, almost bored. Just as he had the night before, Lawrence rushed out of the apartment soon after they'd finished their business. He did so again the following night. From this pattern I deduced that there was a girlfriend waiting for him back home. Paula knew. Yes, she must have known, because she never protested when he sat up to put his pants back on. They simply kissed good-night and he was off.

The affair maintained a steady pace for three weeks, then it abruptly halted. She came home alone two, three, then four nights in a row, and switched back to her routine of bath, wine, and reading. The change didn't appear to bother her.

A week or so later I was out for a Wednesday evening stroll. Paula had just left for work, but I still took the precaution of beard and glasses. My destination was a little boutique on lower Madison that had just acquired a Fabergé egg for display from an anonymous Russian dealer. A forest-green-enamel shell draped with twenty-four-carat appointments, it rested atop a miniature sterling-silver chariot. The boutique displayed the little treasure in the front window behind double security glass and two armed guards. I stood outside the store, my mouth agape at the egg's crippling beauty. Such detailed perfection! Its power froze me there on the sidewalk. But a young, bickering couple shattered my reverie as they yelled back and forth at full volume on their way past me.

"You knew the deal," the woman shouted. "I told you straight out. If you cheated and you told me, I'd leave you. If you cheated and didn't tell me, I'd kill you. Just be happy you told me. You're still alive, right?"

"But I'm telling you because I don't want you to leave me."

"Get the fuck away from me! You want me to call the police? You want to make a scene?"

By then I was following a few feet behind them. When I got a glimpse of his profile I was struck dumb. Lawrence. I turned on my heel and merged back into the stream of pedestrians. I will never get used to the uncanny New York phenomenon whereby one can live in the city for years and never run into an acquaintance except at the most inopportune moments. It's as if the metropolis has a pattern of destiny worked out for its residents. At any time it can open the doors of its cabs or restaurants to reveal the person it wants you to find.

I returned at once to the apartment. At four-twenty in the morning, Paula brought him home with her. She sat in the armchair while he paced around the living room. He was agitated, barely making eye contact with her, gesturing as he spoke. Finally, she'd had all she could take of his ranting. She stood, took him by the hand, and led him to bed. But now the strangest thing of all. They began to kiss. She removed her shirt and tossed it to the floor. Right away I knew something wasn't right. He was hesitant, not touching her, and in turn it caused her to recoil. The kissing died down. He walked back into the living room and rubbed his face with his hands. Paula didn't follow him. She sat on the edge of the bed, leaning forward, and played with her hair. Right there I snapped her picture, and I realized where I'd seen the same pose. "Interior." She was unconsciously mimicking the woman in the painting. The confused lover after the failed attempt at passion. But Paula's pose was more of disgust. She now knew that Lawrence had used her to get out of his relationship. For a long time she just shook her head and almost seemed to laugh.

Finally, she got up and drew a bath. Lawrence called out a lame good-bye that she probably didn't hear over the running water, and let himself out. Waiting for the tub to fill, she took off her clothes and underwear—matching, beige top and bottom—went to the window fully naked, and gazed down at the street. Suddenly, as if she'd forgotten a roast in the oven, she darted out of the bedroom. I struggled to keep up with her, adjusting the tripod to the living room position. I found her back in the hall closet. In no time she had dug the metal box out again and was studying the hinges on its back. Then she fetched the Phillips screwdriver that I keep in a kitchen drawer, took the box to the bed, and began undoing the hinges. Six simple screws. I cursed a blue streak, for I was out of film. There was no way to reload without missing the big moment. She hesitated before lifting the lid off, the same way one pauses before tossing a coin into a fountain. Then *voilà!* She stared down at my triumph. Two empty foil chocolate wrappers and her Polaroid picture.

Perhaps for a fleeting second it dawned on her that she was the pawn in my larger game and not the player. But then she buried this disturbing notion with more plausible explanations. My guess, and it is just a guess, is that she made herself believe I had developed a secret crush on her. That the contents of the box represented hidden desire, a clandestine shrine to her. Perhaps she even took pity on the version of me she'd constructed in her mind. Art as deception. Thank you very much, Cecilia Muñoz.

That night she searched the apartment another time, making sure to hit every possible hiding place for more clues to explain the metal box. Nothing. From that day forward she became more obsessive about locking the chain on the front door.

I hadn't meant the contents of the box to be read in any one way. Art must be interpreted, not simply deciphered. If sheer communication was my goal, I'd probably just make obscene phone calls. What's important is that the artist senses an influence upon the audience, not that he or she controls them. In my own work, the multiplicity of responses in each of my subjects always struck me as one of the more interesting aspects of the sublet piece. No doubt the same desire for unpredictability led me to take on that conundrum of a girl from India.

●

I'd faced a bit of a quandary when it came time to prepare the metal box for Maya. There were no chocolate wrappers and no Polaroid to personalize her private installation. I lay in bed each night trying to come up with the perfect ingredients before I finally hit upon what I thought was an inspired solution. Three mornings before her stay began, I went to a health food store down the block. In all the years I'd lived in the neighborhood, I'd never set foot inside the place. It had a funny smell. Incense, or pet rodents, or the bulk grains, I couldn't tell which. I approached a middle-aged woman, her ratty hair tied up with a ratty scarf. "Can you help me find a decent chocolate substitute?" I asked. "I have a friend who's allergic."

"You already probably know about carob, right?"

"Carob?"

"Right over here. That's the stuff you should get. Tastes better than chocolate, if you ask me."

"You don't say. What, it's sweetened with honey or something?"

"Would you like to try a piece?"

I spared my taste buds the insult. After all, the flavor wasn't what really mattered. I needed a prop. I bought a single circular piece of it, an inch in diameter. It was even wrapped in a silver foil that nearly matched the chocolate balls I normally use. As for the absence of the photograph, I glued a four-inch square of mirror to the bottom of the box, so that when, or if, she opened the lid, she'd be staring down at herself. On top of the mirror I placed the wrapped carob, as if to say, "Now you can indulge yourself without fear." I knew it was all a bit of a gamble, but it was the best I could come up with. I just had to hope that if she opened the box, she'd recognize that the contents were arranged specially for her.

Back then I had foreseen a successful summer. Little did I know that just days into her stay I'd start to forget what Maya even looked like. I searched my memory for her features and got as far as skin color and the bindi. In a supreme act of willpower, I forced the whole notion of Mara Thompson out of my conscious thoughts. A red herring, I told myself. If it was Maya, and she was trying to throw someone off, it didn't involve me. The same held true for all I'd learned about the name. The Evil One, Temptress, or god of whatever might be roaming the Harlem streets that very moment, but, as far as I knew, creatures of such lofty titles didn't tend to put down cash for a sublet.

I assured myself the old man made a simple mistake, misunderstood my description, or, better still, another hotel guest wore the bindi. Lots of Indian people live in London, after all. Why not more than one tourist in the same New York hotel at once? More than likely, Maya sat on a prime piece of Hamptons beach, reading a magazine and sipping iced tea.

Day six of her torturous stay. I woke up with clogged sinuses and a fierce headache. I badly needed to get out of my stuffy apartment and into the fresh air, so I headed back to the Cecilia Muñoz show to inspect it without Henry's grousing. I took a cab through the wet streets to the Modern. Just as I pulled up, the rain receded. A small crowd of people took the opportunity to leave the shelter of the museum's entryway.

Black hair, a glimpse at a woman's profile. I bolted forward. A brown dress, sandals. Maya. Heading toward Fifth Avenue. Maya! I threw a twenty at the cabdriver and didn't wait for change.

My pulse sputtered. Ten paces back. The right height, the right hair, the right clothes, but could I be sure? What about the Bhagavad Gita? Should I trust my senses? She turned left onto Fifth Avenue. A river of people. I lost her for a second, found her again. I kept far enough behind that I never got a clear shot at her face. She carried a camera in her right hand. A disposable. The foot traffic stopped at the corner of Fifty-fifth Street. I angled my way to get a look but wasn't minding the other pedestrians and ran smack into an elderly lady. "Not very considerate, are you?" the young businesswoman next to me scolded.

"At least say excuse me!" a man in a construction outfit shouted.

"Excuse me," I mumbled. It was terrifying. People staring at me, the noise. Maya so close. I ducked down and scurried off in the other direction.

"Get a life, you fucking jerk!" the man yelled after me.

After half a block I doubled back. The lunchtime crowd filled the entire sidewalk for as far as I could see. Finding her again seemed impossible. I checked the storefronts of the chic clothing boutiques, zigzagging my way through the hostile stream of pedestrians. Amazing how many people along this stretch of Fifth Avenue take pictures with disposable cameras. It must be one of the most photographed parts of New York.

"Watch it asshole!" a cabdriver yelled when I stepped in front of his car.

"Sorry. Excuse me," I said in a disguised, low-pitched voice. I must have looked like a madman. It went on this way for two blocks, until I was certain I wouldn't see her again. Just as I was about to give up, the crowd shifted and I found her on the far corner of Fifty-seventh Street. She stood taking a picture of Bergdorf Goodman department store. It's housed in a stately old limestone building, photogenic enough I suppose, but not extraordinary. It always delights me to see what tourists deem as worthy of capturing on film. Maybe Maya bought a dress there, I thought. Perhaps she just liked the austere architecture.

The light changed and I slowly crossed the street, giving her enough time to finish taking the picture. She moved on to the Plaza hotel at Fifty-ninth, where she took another shot. Then we entered Central Park. Groups of businesspeople carried lunch bags with them and sat on the benches by the water. The farther we went into the heart of the park, the fewer people we encountered.

Walking the same road the horse-drawn carriages use, we passed the skating rink. The sun came out, and the heat, kept in check by the morning showers, came back with it. Maya clicked off a half dozen photos: footbridge, horse and carriage, Rollerbladers. Christ, I thought, if I only had a camera, a disposable even. I ordered myself to record the scene into memory. The way the fabric clung to her back and accentuated her slender waist. How she let her heels glide along the ground as she strolled. From a brown woven handbag she removed a pair of wayfarer-type sunglasses. Capture every movement, fix her in your mind.

We went along at a leisurely pace, deeper into the center of the park. I grew more and more nervous. For a good two or three minutes we were the only two people on the road. All she'd have to do was turn around and I'd be spotted. Reluctantly, I let the distance between us widen. Sweat trickled down my sides. I was absurdly overdressed for such a hike in the middle of summer. Coveralls, the hat, ankle-high work boots, not to mention the beard.

She headed toward a clearing in the trees, beyond which

lay the Great Lawn—a vast open space bigger than a few football fields put together, where the city occasionally holds concerts. I stopped at the fringe, beneath the canopy of trees, and watched her walk straight into the wide open center of the field, between two softball diamonds. Sunbathers and picnickers dotted the grassy expanse for as far as I could see. An outfielder taunted a batter, "He's got nothing. Can't hit. Strikeout coming, strikeout coming."

Dormant for so long, the sickness, the phobia, swooped down and blindsided me. Paralysis stiffened over my joints. "He's gonna whiff. Strikeout King. Three pitches." My heart pounded in the pit of my stomach. No earthly way I could follow her. I took one last look at her trajectory and made a rough calculation as to where she'd exit the clearing. Then I closed my eyes, turned around, and started running around the wooded periphery. When I tried to sneak a look across the field, the nausea felled me and I had to stop, clamp my eyes shut, and start over. On top of it all, I'm not in the best physical shape, and I had to pause to catch my breath several times. Too much lost time. When I reached the other side, she was nowhere to be found. I didn't have the strength to search the lawn to see if she'd stopped to sit. Instead, I faced the other way and scoured the trickle of children and parents as they headed back toward Central Park West and the solace of tall buildings and concrete. I'd lost her again.

"If a traveler doesn't meet with one who's better," I recited as I started down the asphalt path leading out of the park, "let her keep to her solitary journey. No companionship with this fool." Five years without an agoraphobic attack. I'd started to believe I'd beaten it. Boundaries. Yet again Maya left me questioning my ability to govern myself. I couldn't shake the sense that she'd led me to the Great Lawn on purpose. That somehow she knew of my weakness and wanted to test it. For the first time, I started to wonder whether Maya wasn't playing me. Who was the artist and who the work of art? Still, there were too many ways to explain it all away. I'd seen her acting like a tourist again. Her physical presence alone was enough to clear my head of more supernatural thoughts.

●

T he thrill of trailing her in the park renewed my vigilance at the eyepiece. At last I felt as though I was getting closer to her. I let myself believe that the sighting would prove just a precursor. But as the afternoon light darkened, and my aperture speed grew longer, I saw how meaningless a victory I'd won. I knew nothing more of her. The same mysteries persisted. Yes, she was still here in New York, but beyond that? These admissions brought on a heavy depression, made worse by the lingering exhaustion and jitters of the anxiety attack. I popped a Valium and passed out on the sofa.

Two hours later I woke up feeling truly awful. No movement across the way. My sneezing worse, I went to the kitchen and took my temperature. One hundred on the dot. It was unwise, but at this moment of weakness I went out for dinner in Little India, the strip of thirty-five odd Indian restaurants that cluster around Sixth Street between First and Second avenues. No doubt the Valium didn't help my judgment.

I'm not a great fan of Indian cuisine, all those stews and overspiced condiments. The real reason I chose this locale must seem perfectly obvious, not to mention ridiculous. Why would Maya want to hang around the mediocre approximations of restaurants from her homeland? When Italians visit New York they don't rush out and eat lesser versions of their country's own dishes in Little Italy. Such was my desperate state.

Barkers lined the streets, attempting to steer passersby into their prospective restaurants. "Right this way. Ten percent discount. The best food right this way. Please try it, sir. Complimentary glass of wine." I selected a place called the Ganges precisely because no one from the establishment approached me.

A man wearing a turban sat in the window, plucking away at a sitar. The strong odor of curry vaguely reminded me of human sweat, and if it weren't for the attentiveness of the maître d' I would have left. "Please, sir. Table for one, sir. Follow me." Garish plastic garlands hung from the low ceiling, and I had to duck on the way to the table. A busboy placed two greasy, waferlike crackers and a glass of water without ice in front of me. I ordered chicken tikka and a cup of hot tea. My head was throbbing and I was regretting leaving the apartment, but just then a rotund woman walked by on her way to the kitchen. She wore the bindi on her forehead, a few centimeters higher up than Maya's. For a fleeting moment I thought I remembered what Maya's face looked like. I savored the pictures in my mind's eye of our afternoon walk. How could I have gotten so close and come up empty? The waiter passed my table. "Can you answer a question for me?" I asked.

"I think so. I will try." He was a very short man dressed in a tuxedo shirt, maroon vest, and clip-on bow tie.

"Tell me about the red dot. The bindi, or the tilaka."

"Oh yes, you know the name."

"Which one do you use?"

"Either one is fine. I prefer bindi, it is the more common. What is it that you would like to know, sir?"

"What does it signify?"

"Marriage, sir."

"Marriage?"

"It is worn by married women. Very common for the last generation."

"Always? What I mean is, is that all that it signifies?"

"No, not always, sometimes men can wear one too, and not all women who wear the bindi are married." A middle-aged couple entered the restaurant and the waiter excused himself to seat them. I flagged him down again on his way to the kitchen.

"What other reasons might someone wear it?"

"Perhaps there could be spiritual reasons."

"Spiritual, yes. I've heard it called the window to the soul. It has something to do with time and space and perception, am I right?"

He laughed nervously. "I'm afraid I cannot help you further. I am not a spiritual man. There might be many reasons that I do not know, but I can say to you that it is also true that many people simply like the bindi as some kind of fashion."

"Fashion!"

"Many people, I'm sure of it. Excuse me, I hear the kitchen bell."

I swore to myself then and there that I wouldn't go back to the library. What good had it done me? "The mystical point outside time and space where the absolute and the phenomenal meet." When I first read that definition of the third eye, I thought surely I'd found the right fit. It matched Maya's description of a window to the soul, but now I had to reconcile myself to the possibility of other interpretations. Perhaps Maya's dot also represented both a spiritual connection *and* a stylish whim. I could spend day after day reading a roomful of books on India's spiritual tradition, on red dots and gods of lust and sin, and might never know if I'd come any closer to understanding her. Without the real Maya in front of me to confirm or refute my findings, the research held little to no use.

I was dizzy and pulled out two antihistamines from my pocket. All this time I'd told myself it was a simple matter of unlocking some mystical clue and I'd understand her, I'd capture her. The third eye, the measuring of the bathtub, the Old Memorial, the old man dying in the library, her repulsion with "Interior." I was worked up into such a confused state that I was incapable of discerning clue from coincidence, hard fact from fiction, premonition from hallucination. She simply had to be staying with the Handsforths. This was not a mystery, I assured myself. Logic would win the day. Sizzling on a hot black platter and wafting a trail of white smoke, the yogurt-and-spice-stained chicken arrived.

●

When I got back home the phone was ringing, and I ran from the elevator so the machine wouldn't pick up. "Hello," I said a little out of breath.

"Hi, it's Henry. What are you doing, exercising?"

"Just walked in from dinner. I was about to call you."

"Why? What's wrong?"

"Nothing's wrong. Aside from the usual. Notice any pretty Indian women loitering around the gallery?"

"You mean your tenant? Jesus, are you telling me she's still not there?"

I paused. "Afraid not. I take it you haven't seen her."

"Hold on, that's my other line beeping." He clicked over. I squatted down in front of my CD collection and began looking for the Kreutzer sonata. Thinking of Paula put me in the mood to hear it. Click again. "Sorry. Some intern at the gallery. Could I come down and help with this and that. All these fucking little details!"

"How is the hanging of the show going?"

"Almost done, thank God. Been a real pain in the ass. There's too many people around. Interns, food delivery, electricians. Impossible to sit quietly and figure out where everything should go. You can't think. I'll be right in the middle of putting one of them up, after an hour of measuring and going up and down the damn ladder, then Dianne will walk in with some shlub. 'Can you come down for a second, Henry. Here's someone you really have to meet.' It's more than annoying. It's exhausting is what it is. Mentally exhausting. If I shake another person's hand, I might just snap."

"You are on edge, aren't you?"

"I'm telling you."

"Should I come down, lend a hand?"

"No, don't. No offense. There's too many people there as it is."

"When's the opening? Thursday, right?"

"Right, Thursday."

"I hope there weren't any disagreements about which paintings to show. Did it go over all right with them?" I sneezed.

"Bless you."

"This damn cold."

"What are you doing with a cold in the middle of July?"

"It's terrible. I think I'm over the worst of it."

"So I probably won't even see you Thursday."

"And why is that?"

"Seeing as how there's a chance your tenant might be there."

"True. Although I did consider going in disguise."

"Sounds too risky."

"You're probably right. Then again, for all I know, she won't even show up."

"How can you be sure?"

"I can't."

"Better sit this one out. Come the week after, when things have died down."

"I was planning on Friday. You sound strange to me,

Henry. Is everything all right? You didn't have any problems with the gallery people, did you?"

"No, Jesus Christ, no. They're real dimwits. Conceited bastards, her more than him. Always talking shit about other galleries like they're the only ones in New York with any taste. And they treat you like they're doing you a favor, because if it's not an Archer-Handsforth show, then what good is it."

"Well in a way they are doing you a favor, Henry. Don't bite the hand . . ."

"I wasn't."

"But you did draw the line about the pictures."

"Yes, for the thousandth time."

"Okay, sorry. Tell me more about Dianne Handsforth. What's she all about?"

"A rich bitch who likes to tell people what to do."

"They say she's quite savvy when it comes to business."

"Is that what they say?"

"And, too, that she made the careers of dozens of the biggest artists of the past twenty years."

"How many biggest artists have we had in the past twenty years?"

"Why are you being so cagey?"

"You asked me what she was like. I'm telling you. I'm not impressed. The woman's a shark. Does she know business? Yes. Does she give a shit about art or artists? I can't tell you for sure. No, my sense is no. This show has me so fucking on edge. It'll probably be a disaster. I should have listened to you. Never should have taken it. If I could, I'd kill it, but it's too late."

"Come on, it can't be that bad."

"It is."

"By chance, has she mentioned her place out in the Hamptons?"

"It's in Sag Harbor. She goes there four or five days a week. Why?"

"Henry, I told you. Maya said Dianne had taken her. That's the whole reason I got so upset in the first place."

"Right, I remember. So you think she might be living out there?"

"It explains her absence."

"If they're that close, you'd better stay away from the opening. There's going to be a party and a dinner afterward. Sounds to me like the kind of thing she'd invite her houseguests to. Listen, I've got to go, I'm meeting a friend for a drink."

"All right, Henry. I expect a full report of the gala. Keep an eye out for Maya."

"I will."

"Tell me honestly. You're not still mad about her flipping your painting around."

"No."

"I mean you wouldn't say anything to her."

"For Christ sake!"

"Henry—"

"You could at least give me a little credit."

"You're right, I'm sorry. I apologize. Just wanted to make sure. Don't be nervous about the show. It'll be fine."

"Thanks."

Why didn't I tell him about Maya in the park? Though we'd been friends for nearly three years, he still didn't know about my agoraphobia. Dr. Wasserstrom and my parents were the only people who did. I confess that in part I felt ashamed of this pseudo-disease. While the concept behind psychosomatic illness made sense intellectually, I never believed it could happen to me. I thought myself too sensible, too entrenched in the world of rational thought, too whole. But now I had to face the fact that my mind was in a divided state. I felt as though I didn't understand—scratch that, like I couldn't trust my subconscious thoughts. It was as if some intruder had taken over my brain's steering wheel. How, then, to wrestle back control of what, by definition, one can't ever really know? The Dr. Wasserstroms of the world may dabble and guess at one's subconscious desires, but they can never know them for certain.

What upset me most of all was that after ten years, I really understood nothing of my own affliction. And if I couldn't explain it to myself, then I certainly didn't have the energy to try to explain it to Henry. The harder admission was that up until the day in the park I had refused to see myself as anything but a passive character in Maya's tale. Though waiting at the camera frustrated me to no end, her failure to appear wasn't a reflection on my abilities. The park changed that. Now my own weakness was to blame for her escape.

That night I lay awake in bed, going over my history with the agoraphobia. There had to be some way to understand and beat it. If it was born in my mind, then the problem would have to die there too. I closed my eyes and recalled the circumstances surrounding the first episode atop the World Trade Center. It had coincided, I realized, with the rise in my artistic obsession with voyeurism. This revelation immediately sent my mind churning. Could there be a causal link between my project and the illness, I wondered, a bit like a side effect from a powerful drug? After all, painters suffer dizziness from oil-based pigment. Sculptors fumble their chisels and gouge their own hands. Why shouldn't this affliction stem from my own creative medium? Viewed as an outgrowth of the artistic process, my bout with the disease suddenly started to make sense.

My artistic interests had focused me inward, into the private realm—the interior of a person, to use the Degas title. Just as the nature photographer disguises himself in camouflage fatigues and sits beneath a duck blind, I, too, set about capturing unsuspecting subjects, and Manhattan's halting architecture offered the ideal setting. The city's claustrophobic layout became not only an important facet of the project but an obsession. My theory, as I talked it through that night, was that somewhere along the way my need for crowded space and urban sight lines grew so great that the prospect of a wide open view of the horizon made me physically ill.

This manner of self-examination went on in my stuffed-up, feverish head until nearly five in the morning, but every time I got close to convincing myself of that grand psychoanalytic discovery, another voice spoke up inside me. Too constructed, it countered. Too convenient. The explanation was nothing more than a delusion brought on by a lack of sleep and a bad cold. I'd uncovered nothing more than my own desperation for an explanation. By dawn I was locked in stalemate with myself. So much for therapy.

●

Wednesday passed without Maya. Thursday passed without Maya. The light in the apartment burned on and on. I ran into the kitchen and pulled out a lightbulb carton. On average, a seventy-five-watt bulb lasted seven hundred and fifty hours. As soon as I started the mathematical calculations, I realized I didn't know how many watts I'd used in the hall fixture, or exactly when I last changed it. "Idiot," I scolded myself.

Miraculously, the dracaena looked as healthy as ever. Leaves still dark green, and they hadn't wilted at all, a fact that gave rise to another paranoid hypothesis. Perhaps she snuck in and watered the plants while I slept. That night I set the alarm at three A.M., got up, and made certain. I pulled a chair in from the living room and fell asleep for restless one-hour stints between glances. Not the best treatment for a cold.

I was now a captive to my home and the camera, but a willing one, because my condition worsened as the illness made its way through my body. A persistent cough shook me, and my fever bounced the mercury up to one hundred and one point three. A variety of medications left me dehydrated and listless so that the simple activities of reading and looking through the camera lens were more than enough to tire me out.

I spent most of the time in bed, listening to a continuous cycle of early-twentieth-century composers, drifting in and out of dreams. I'd wake, crawl out of bed, check the camera, then get back under the covers. Thursday night I took an especially large dose of cold medication to make sure that I'd put myself out. I must have really overdone it, for a black, dreamless sleep ensued. I came to at one in the afternoon, covered in sweat. The fever had broken, down to ninety-nine. My back and leg muscles had tightened in the night, and as I passed the mirror, I noticed I was walking with the same limping posture I affect in my disguise routine. I took a hot shower and made myself an espresso. My head began to clear. I picked up the phone and dialed Henry. "Dying to know how it went. Give me a call. I'm better today. Think I'll go check out the gallery."

The weather was beautiful. Eighty degrees and sunny, only a trace of humidity. Good to be outside again. I felt like I'd been away from the city for weeks. To avoid sniffling and fussing with the beard in public, I popped two more antihistamines on the short walk to Archer-Handsforth.

A little rush of pride tickled me when I saw Henry's name stenciled in bold black letters on the outside of the gallery, but this was swiftly snuffed out. There in the front window, plain for all to see, was one of the paintings I'd expressly forbidden him to show. Victoria standing at the window. The rage sizzled inside my skull. I entered bracing for the worst and was duly rewarded. Dammit, Henry! Every single one. Every Victoria we'd gone over without exception.

A fresh-faced, blond gallery girl approached me. "If you have any questions," she said.

"If I needed your damn help, I'd have asked for it," I barked.

Her lips trembled, and she turned away without another word. Out of the corner of my eye I saw her picking up the phone. I remember the sensation of hot blood pulsing in my temples. "Please forgive my rude behavior," I called as I strode out the door.

Back on the street, I paced without direction, plotting the demise of the paintings. A can of black paint and a brush to blot out all traces of my building, but landing in jail didn't seem like the smartest move. Besides, something told me that the damage had already been done. I gathered my wits and ran back home.

Henry's machine picked up my frantic call. "You'd better talk to me as soon as possible," I said, and slammed the receiver down. At the telephoto lens I found both her bedroom and the living room empty and dark. Yes, dark. My face muscles tensed, and I started panting through my nose. The hall light was out, leaving the foyer shrouded in shadows. "Henry! This better have nothing to do with you and your paintings," I babbled. "Henry, Henry, Henry. You are so weak-willed. What more befits you, pity or disgust? Disgust. Definitely disgust."

My judgment had not completely abandoned me, for I made sure to snap a few pictures of the darkened hallway. I was in such a state that I didn't trust my own senses and wanted physical evidence to explain my motive for the crazy thing I was about to do. The question pulsed behind my eyes. I had to know whether the bulb had expired naturally or been turned off. I pulled the baseball cap down over my brow, put the sunglasses on, and reached for the keys to the rental apartment.

I rounded the corner, past the bodega and the shoe repair shop. Right up to the front door. Two at a time, I bounded up the steps until I stood facing apartment number five. The dead bolt and then the door handle lock. I was in. The familiar smell attested to how little the place had changed. No lingering perfumes or leftover curry. Suddenly, the thought of seeing the light switch frightened me very much. The idea of confirming it one way or the other terrified me. How strange to see my hand write these words, for I always thought not knowing was the worst part.

I averted my eyes from the switch and stepped into the kitchen. The dishes were all put away, and the refrigerator lay as bare as I had left it. The answering machine light blinked at me. One message. From her, I thought. She's toying with you. I took a breath and pushed the button. "You're a bastard," a female voice said. "A heartless, unfeeling bastard. I don't care who you think you are. You and your fancy apartment. It doesn't mean you're better than the rest of us. I just wanted to call and make sure you knew that, you lying sack of shit." I exhaled. Not Maya, but familiar. Yes, Eva Wilson. On instinct I hit the erase button, then realized my mistake. Think, Mr. Jefferson, think! If Maya came back, she'd know someone had been there. Too late, there was no way to reset. Why had she saved the message in the first place? Or had she? Maybe it had just come in. Sadly out of date, my answering machine doesn't inform you of the day or time of the call. Keep moving, I told myself.

Again I avoided looking at the light switch as I walked through the foyer and into the living room. No signs of her presence. No luggage, discarded shopping bags, or debris. In the bedroom I opened the drawer and inspected *My Secret Life*. The bookmark parted the same two pages. In the bathroom I got down on my knees and ran my fingertips along the bottom of the tub to try to detect a trace of soap residue. "Unbelievable," I muttered. "Not a shred of evidence. Nothing to measure."

On the way to the hall closet I searched the ground for a stray hair, powder from a compact, lint, a coin, anything. Finally, the urge to look at the light switch won out. I turned, stared. Down. Off position. Proof she'd been there again. I stepped over and clicked it on. The damn bulb lit up and mocked me. Why had she turned it off? What significance should I read into this simple action? I cursed the timing of my cold. Of all the nights to drug myself! She'd had a full twelve hours to come and go.

Three knocks came from the front door. Three clear knocks. Three quick knocks. Urgent, demanding knocks. A sneeze was coming on. Seconds passed. A droplet of sweat trickled down my side. More seconds. My heart rate fast and climbing. Maya, could it be? Why didn't she just let herself in with the key? I walked softly on my tennis-shoe soles. Four long steps over the creaking hardwood floor. Three more knocks. Louder, faster. My eye to the peephole. "Henry!" I exploded. "What in God's name?" I threw the door open and confronted him. "Explain yourself."

"I was on my way to your place. Saw you going in."

"Have you been following me?"

"No, of course not. I told you, I was on my way to your house. I called your name, but you didn't hear me. This isn't the time to argue. Jesus Christ, do you know the risk you're taking? What the hell are you doing here?"

"The risk *I'm* taking. That's fine, Henry. That's just dandy."

He started whispering. "No, listen to me. Maya could show up any second. Let's get out of here before something bad happens."

"Something bad already has happened, Henry. Now step inside."

"What the fuck are you talking about? We can't stay here. Have you lost your mind?"

"Get out of the hall."

He checked the stairwell. "If she comes back, it's not my fault. You just remember that for the record." He stepped across the threshold.

I shut the door behind him, locked the dead bolt, and

followed him into the living room. "I've just come from your big show."

"Now don't start. I was coming to explain. I've been meaning to tell you, I just needed the right time."

"The right time?"

"I'll explain the whole thing, but not here. It's too dangerous."

"How I ever trusted you . . . You're really quite a crafty little liar, Henry. Amazing. After all I've done for you—"

"Don't start that again."

"Yes I will start that again, Henry. Yes, I will. Really, I'm in awe at this moment. I can't wait to hear what sort of lame excuses you've got stockpiled."

"They were the paintings Dianne Handsforth wanted. I tried. I told her no, but she said it was a choice between going with all of them or forgetting the whole show."

"So you lied to me."

"Did you hear what I just said? She was going to kill the show!"

"You little ingrate! If it wasn't for me, you wouldn't have a show in the first place."

"Bullshit. Fuck you. That's bullshit."

"No? Your gratitude overwhelms me. You don't mean to tell me you think you would have gotten this far without my help?"

"Right," he sneered.

"I was the one, Henry, who showed you your mistakes. Me, not some has-been instructor at the academy. You were nowhere before I came along and—"

"Fuck you and your help. You didn't make me. You didn't paint my paintings. I'll move out of the studio in a second, and I don't need your photos either or your free meals. Listen to yourself! You're a fucking control freak. A total control freak."

"And it seems you're nothing but an ungrateful piece of white trash."

His face flushed red, and he took a threatening step toward me.

"What are you going to do, Henry? Beat me up?"

He clenched his fists and stopped short. "Let's go. We have to get out of here. Immediately. Come on, I'm serious. All this fighting isn't important."

"I find it very important, Henry. I find it very important that you so casually betrayed my trust, and then have the sheer . . . what . . . the sheer audacity to try to paint yourself as some kind of victim. That's really something. So please tell me why it is you think this is all not important. Go on. I want to hear it."

He closed his eyes and shook his head to tell me I was crazy, then went to the window and checked the sidewalk. "I met her last night at the opening," he said as he looked down at the street.

"Met who?"

"Maya."

"You what? Stop right there. You did what?" I began pacing the living room floor. "Henry, do you remember when I first gave you Laura's pictures?" He avoided my eyes. "Do you?"

"Yes I remember. Jesus Christ, do we have to do this?"

"Then I assume you also remember the specific guidelines that I laid out for you. And of those guidelines there was a single point. A single point I attempted to impress upon you above all others, was there not? Was there not, Henry?"

"I didn't break that rule."

"I'm sorry, what did you say?"

"I didn't break that rule. She introduced herself to me, I didn't want to talk to her. I was just standing there."

"No doubt once again you're completely innocent, Henry. One more time an innocent. Why didn't you just walk away?"

"Quiet!" he spat out, and put his index finger to his lips. "Footsteps."

I froze. No sound save the horn of a passing car. He pointed to the front door. I tiptoed through the foyer and peered out the peephole into the empty hall. "There's no one there, Henry. You're hearing things."

"Check outside."

"Henry, other people live in the building. It was probably Mrs. Adolfo downstairs. Now enough stonewalling. Let's get back to your nice little story. Even if it did happen as you say, that she introduced herself to you, why didn't you call me immediately? This isn't some tiny detail. You knew I'd been searching for her. I mean really, Henry! What haven't you done wrong here?"

He turned away from the window but didn't answer. Then he puffed his cheeks as though trying to push out a defeated whistle.

"What is wrong with you? What did I do? What could I have possibly done to make you feel you had to abuse my trust this way?"

"Nothing happened. You've got to believe me."

"*Happened?* What do you mean, happened? I should hope that nothing happened. Jesus. Henry, I—" I'd never felt such anger. My brain inched toward overload. I turned and clapped my hands as hard as I could in an attempt to restart my thoughts. "Are you hearing yourself? I wonder, can you honestly hear what it is that you're saying? Speak slowly, all right? Don't get ahead of yourself. Don't let your mouth outrun your wee little country-boy brain, because I want to hear every bit of it, start to finish. You say she walked up to you at the opening."

He glared at me with almost as much fury in his eyes as I threw back at him. "Yes."

"And she was alone?"

"Yes. She introduced herself. Can I *please* just tell you over at your place? Please?"

I stepped toward him and got right up in his unshaven face. "Now, Henry. Now. How did it happen? Don't skimp on the detail."

"Christ!" He put his hands up between us and backed away from me. "All right, you want it now, I'll give it to you now. I was standing in the corner, half watching, nervous. You know how I get at those things."

"How far away was she when you noticed her?"

"I don't know, twenty feet."

"You caught her eye?"

"Yes."

"And you recognized her from that afternoon at my apartment, correct?"

"Yes."

"What was her facial expression?"

"I don't know, normal."

"What do you mean, normal? Was she smiling, was she upset, what? Detail, detail!"

"It's hard to say. She didn't look happy, but then she didn't seem upset either. Headed straight for me, that's what I remember most, and she never stopped looking in my eyes. Then she got close and I said hello."

"Did you shake her hand?"

"No."

"What was she wearing?"

"I can't remember."

"Henry! Snap out of it. A dress? Pants?"

"Pants and a shirt. I don't know what color. Beige maybe."

"I want you to think very hard. Did she have a red dot on her forehead?"

"Yes. I'm positive. The thing you told me about. I remember that specifically."

"Bravo, Henry. Well done. So you said hello, then what?"

"She said hello back and then there was a little pause and then she said, 'I wanted to have a moment with the artist.' "

"Stop. She knew you were the artist. How?"

"People were talking to me. It was kind of obvious I was the guy who did the work."

"How did she look when she said that? Her facial expression. This is crucial."

"You know, serious. Not angry, but . . ."

"But what?"

"Not altogether happy. Kind of purposeful-looking. That's the best I can describe it."

"Purposeful-looking? You're something, Henry. You know that? You tell one hell of a lousy story, farm boy."

"Shut up! Just shut the fuck up. I'm trying."

"Well keep trying. What happened next?"

"We stood there. And she asked how long I had been a painter. I told her, and then she asked me where I was from. And I asked her the same. She said somewhere in India."

"Banaras?"

"I think so. That sounds right. So I asked how long she was here for, and she said, 'Just a short time.' Then I asked where was she staying and she said, 'Not far away.' "

"Was she more specific?"

"No."

"Henry! You didn't push her? You just left it at that?"

"Well it's not like I could say 16 Spring Street, perhaps? Apartment five?"

"But 'Not far away' could be anywhere. It could be the Upper West Side for all we know. It could be New Jersey. You learned nothing from 'Not far away.' Nothing."

"Wait, she told me she hadn't seen any other parts of the States besides Manhattan and Long Island, so you can forget Jersey. Makes perfect sense too."

"What makes perfect sense?"

"Long Island. That's got to be where she's been up till now. You were right."

"Did she tell you that? Did she say specifically she'd been sleeping in the Hamptons for the past two weeks straight?"

"No, but it has to be."

"What else did you talk about?"

"Okay, this is important. She starts looking at the painting behind me."

"Which one?"

" 'Woman at Rest.' "

"Another that you weren't supposed to show."

"Are you going to let me finish this?"

"Finish."

"She took a step toward it. Now I remember, she was wearing a skirt and sandals. I think a blue shirt, like a T-shirt, you know, a fancy kind. She had a stud in her nostril, gold. Some other jewelry."

"Suddenly you're Mr. Detail."

He ignored me. "Then she says, 'These are not quite as realistic as I expected.' And then, 'They have an artificial quality about them.' I think that was it. I thought she was going to keep talking, so I waited. I thought maybe she'd say whether or not she liked the work. We just kind of stood there, looking at the painting. It was awkward. She was awkward. I was pretty nervous too."

"How was she awkward?"

"Maybe it was more me than her. I wasn't happy to see her there, I can tell you that."

"I take it you didn't ask what she meant by 'expecting'?"

"Meaning what?"

"Meaning why should she be expecting anything at all about your paintings? Wait, of course. Dianne probably described them to her. Continue, you were standing there like a half-wit, letting the silence build."

"What was I supposed to do?"

"Ask her name for starters."

"I knew her name already."

I felt like choking him. "That's right, excuse me, you're right. You already knew her name. Silly of me. You knew her name so there was no reason to ask. Please continue."

"Finally, after like five minutes of standing there, she says, 'All in all, very intriguing portraits. You have captured something, I'll grant you that much.'"

"Those were her exact words?"

"You've certainly captured something, that much I'll grant you."

"Hold on. What was the exact line? 'You have captured something, I'll grant you that much' or 'You've certainly captured something, that much I'll grant you'?"

"What the hell's the difference?"

"The difference is one was something she said and one was not. I don't care to fill my head any further with false details. Do you understand? Believe me, I wish I didn't have to rely on you to create this picture in my head. It makes me more than a tad nervous that you can't remember the specifics of such a crucial moment. Just one more blow to your already damaged credibility—"

" 'You have captured something, I'll grant you that much,' " he interrupted.

"You're certain."

"Certain."

I thought for a moment. "Did you respond?"

"I was going to. I started to ask if that meant she liked them, but Dianne Handsforth interrupted with a critic she wanted me to meet, and when I turned back around, Maya was gone."

"And?"

"He was a banker, some Wall Street guy."

"I don't care about him, you idiot. What happened next with Maya?"

He pursed his lips.

"You'd better have more, Henry. This can't be where your story ends. You had really better hope that there's more."

"Stop yelling."

"I will not stop yelling!"

"She left. I didn't see her again. Understand? Maybe that's not what you want to hear, maybe you'd like to try and twist it, change a word here or there, put your Ivy-League-millionaire spin on it and make it come out better for you. Well too fucking bad. It's done. She left. You can't throw your money at this and change it—"

It all happened very fast, like a spring-loaded release. I landed a hard punch square on his left eye. He was stunned, more out of surprise than pain. But in the next second he retaliated, hurling himself on top of me and knocking me to the ground. The blows came in a flurry to my neck, shoulders, forehead, and then, with a crowning finish, the whole of my nose. I felt the cracking sound and then the moisture, but I didn't realize I was bleeding until I saw Henry's expression change. I was on my back, looking up at him. Slowly, the focus returned to my eyes. As he got off me, I discovered something else.

"Jesus," he said. "I'm sorry. You shouldn't have hit me. I'm sorry."

"Get out. Go!"

"No, really. I didn't mean to get you so bad. You just—"

"What a wretch you are. A lousy wretch."

"You're bleeding all over the place. You're bleeding on the rug."

"Get out, Henry, before I punch you again." I pulled out my handkerchief and held it to my nose.

"I'll wait downstairs. If she comes, I'll ring the buzzer as a warning."

"She's long gone, Henry. Look." From the ground I pointed to the mantel. "Interior" had been flipped back around and rehung. "She's not coming, you moron. Get it through your backwater Cro-Magnon skull."

"Fuck off." At last he let me be.

Maya had left for good. It all added up. If she wasn't planning on leaving, then why turn the painting back around? The light switch showed the same conviction. She had restored the apartment to the way she'd found it, because she wasn't coming back. Screw the plants. Henry's story corroborated as much. Clearly, she had been toying with him at the opening. Regardless of the exact wording, the gist of her comments about portraits and capturing and realism gave her away. She figured it out. How long ago, I couldn't say. That must have been the reason she stayed away, so as not to be captured herself.

I stared up at the ceiling, thinking my fate had been sealed. Perhaps the police were on their way that very moment. Maybe they'd stop at the gallery first and give me a few last moments of peace. I resigned myself to the arrest and shut my eyes. But after a minute or so of lying there on the carpet, the feeling struck me that one last detail remained. I got up and started unpacking the closet, throwing the blankets and suitcases out onto the hall floor. Finally, I reached the metal box and brought it into the kitchen. The key trembled in my hand as I undid the lock. I raised the lid. The wrapped carob was still there. The mirror, too, but in the center of it she had painted a small circular third eye in a deep red pigment. Looking down at my reflection, I positioned the bindi to the appointed place on my soiled forehead and saw clearly my premonition. As if it had fallen from the third eye, a crimson tear trickled down the bridge of my nose.

Madness took hold. Gone all foresight and reason. I lifted the box above my head and slammed it down to the ground. The mirror shattered, but I wasn't through. I needed it destroyed, better yet to never have existed. In one frenzied motion I snatched it up again and headed to the front door. I stomped out into the hall and hurled the container down the garbage chute. It scraped its way along the sides of the metal passage and landed with a satisfying thud in the basement Dumpster. Stuttering incoherent half-words, I hurried back into the apartment and locked the dead bolt with unsteady hands.

Three days later I was at my kitchen table, stirring sugar into a demitasse of espresso. My face bore the reminders of Henry's outburst: a dark purple bruise beneath my left eye and a white gauze bandage across the bridge of my nose. I looked much worse than I felt, and it shocked me to see my face in the mirror. A precarious calm presided over my mental state. The police hadn't yet banged on my door yelling about a warrant for my arrest. Yet, I told myself, yet. Now certain she'd fled, the temptation to look through the camera ceased, and I no longer reached for the disguise when I left the apartment. My thoughts never strayed from her for long. I started trying to piece together these strange events into some kind of theory and quickly found I had a long way to go before it coalesced into anything remotely coherent. In time, I assured myself, the mystery of Maya would come to make sense.

I downed the coffee and picked up the morning *Times*, flipping straight to the Arts section. Right there, the front page! A glowing review of Henry's show. I was stunned. Some bits I read aloud out of sheer disbelief.

> In Mr. Magnin's work, one senses an overt stylistic fascination with the Impressionists, namely Manet. The strength of his paintings, however, does not lie in their

impressive technique alone, but is rooted in the subtle
fictions of his subject matter. Employing a razor-sharp
ironic tone, he has taken on the complex topic of voyeurism's relationship to art. . . .

At once sinister and playful, Mr. Magnin's work
examines the tricky boundary between public and private space by using a single redundant setting: women as
seen through the windows of an apartment. It is as if he
is asking the question What differentiates the aesthetic
criteria we use to evaluate a work of art from the way we
look at everyday life?

By the time I finished reading I was laughing so hard that
tears were dripping down my cheeks. Such a coup! A publicist
couldn't have written a better notice. I picked up the phone and
called Henry. It was the first time I'd spoken with him since the
blowout. "Is this Mr. Magnin?" I said. "Mr. Henry Magnin, the
famous artist?"

"What do you want?"

"Please, Henry. It's all right. Can you meet me this evening, say six o'clock?"

He didn't reply right away. "You sure you want to?"

"The little café on Jane Street, neutral ground. Take it as a
peace offering."

"I'll be ready to move out by the first of the month."

"Not necessary."

"Yes it is."

"Just meet me. We'll work things out."

"Six o'clock."

Thick humidity packed the evening air. As I walked along
the crowded streets, people made sure to sneak little glances at
my bruises. No doubt they took me for the victim of a mugging.
Henry sat at an outdoor table and stood up when he saw me

coming. He looked much sharper than usual. Black T-shirt tucked in—yes, tucked in—to a pair of relatively clean khaki pants. My God, he had even shaved!

"Good evening," I said. "Don't you look well groomed."

"Are you all right? How do you feel?"

"Remarkably well considering the vicious beating you gave me. Sit down." He winced as his eyes roamed over my face, and I realized that in the back of my mind I must have wanted him to see me this way. "It's amazing that you don't so much as have a hint of swelling where I hit you. Truly amazing. I must be more of a weakling than I thought." The waitress arrived and I ordered two glasses of champagne. "I've come to congratulate you. Just read the review."

He looked at me sideways, uncertain of my sincerity. "You're not angry about it?"

"I'm happy for your career. Even if the writer completely misrepresented your motives."

"Could you believe that crap? He thought I was trying to be ironic."

"I told you they'd want to have a hook."

"But I hate irony. I know it doesn't matter. What a jackass! But get this, I heard from the gallery this afternoon. They sold seven paintings today. Seven!"

"Power of the press. I hope they upped the price."

"They certainly did."

"Bravo!"

We laughed, and then suddenly he turned very serious. "I need to tell you something."

"Sounds important."

"It is. I'm moving out. I'm sorry. I got another place. I'm giving my notice."

"Now would you stop with that nonsense. You do not have

to move. All is forgiven, you big dolt. What do you mean, you've got another place?"

"A live-work studio. Just a couple blocks from here."

"In SoHo?"

"On Mercer."

"But you . . . What? How did you find it, through the newspaper? An ad?"

"A Realtor friend of Dianne Handsforth's."

"You paid a Realtor! Henry, I could have found you another place, and without the fee. Jesus, you sell a few paintings and suddenly you think you're John Paul Getty? I thought you hated SoHo. Too pretentious, you said, too precious for a real artist."

"I'm sorry."

"Stop saying you're sorry for Christ sake. Boy, you really are full of surprises these days. It's like I don't even know you at all."

The waitress returned with the champagne, but we ignored the glasses and let them bubble away in silence on the white tablecloth. None of the toasts I'd prepared about bygones seemed appropriate any longer.

"I need my own place," he said at last. "I need to do it alone."

"Meaning what, Henry? No more photos? No more partnership?"

"No more photos, no more free dinners, no apartment. And I know what you're going to say and it's not like that. I am grateful for what you did."

"Well now—"

"Don't. Don't interrupt. I just got out of control. I know that. I can see that now. Showing the paintings was way out of line. Lying and hitting you."

"Is this all because of our little row? Henry, I'm trying to tell you, what I came here to tell you before you started in with your announcement is that I forgive you for what you did."

"It's not just the fight. It shouldn't have ever gotten as far as the fight. The whole thing, the whole arrangement. Yes, it helped me, but I need to do it on my own from here on out."

"Admittedly, I was being pretty nasty. Calling you white trash and all that."

"Are you even listening to me? It's not just about the fight. I'm . . ."

"Just say it already."

"It's about independence. About not having to answer to anybody, about not worrying about disappointing anybody. If I fuck up in the future, it'll be just me fucking up."

A tall blond woman wearing a flouncy floral-patterned skirt passed by walking her black standard poodle. The sniffing dog knocked into the far leg of our table, causing it to lurch. Henry and I reached for the glasses. "Jules!" the woman cried. "Bad dog! I'm very sorry. Did you spill? Can I buy you another?"

"We're fine," Henry said. The woman smiled at him and apologized again. We both turned and followed her for a few paces with our eyes.

"Nice dog," I said.

He laughed.

"Listen to me, Henry. If you insist on leaving, I won't try to stop you."

"You couldn't. It's a done deal. I already signed the lease."

"Jesus. That bad, huh? And you say the partnership's finished too?"

"I think it's better this way."

"Too overbearing, was I? Too controlling?"

"Maybe it's more me than you."

"No, that's all right, Henry. You don't have to water any of it down. I suppose it's my nature. It just seems like such a shame. I mean, you were really making progress with this last batch. You don't want to quit now that you're so close."

"Stop."

"Right. But if you change your mind, I've got plenty of shots you haven't done yet."

"I'll keep it in mind." We didn't speak for a few minutes. Henry chipped away at the white paint on his chair with his thumbnail. I lost myself in the rising pattern of bubbles in my champagne.

"So it's official," I finally said. "The artistic partnership is hereby dissolved." I lifted my glass and he reluctantly drank. "Still friends, aren't we? Or do I have to make another toast?"

"That's up to you. After the way I acted, I wouldn't blame you if you didn't want to."

"Hello? Henry? Are you there? You're forgiven. How many times do I have to say it?"

"Just like that?"

"Big of me, no?" I winked and took another drink.

"You're acting strange today."

"Go with it. If I am, it's not doing you any harm."

"Guess you haven't heard anything from Maya."

"No. Listen to me, Henry, you're not to blame for Maya's disappearance, if that's what you think, and that's precisely why I'm so quick to reconcile."

"That's nice of you, but—"

"Now let me finish. After you left the apartment, I sat there in the living room all night long, thinking. Me and Thérèse and Laurent, thinking it over. I get little flashes, blurry little pictures of her. It's like waking up and almost remembering a dream. Then I start to review what actually happened. I'll admit, it's hard for me to get my mind around how and why. Part of me thinks that I'm going to find that one little thing that will fit it all into place. Click, and I'll understand."

"Listen, you can't—"

"Let me talk for a minute. I'm not finished."

"Sorry."

"The more I go over it in my head, the more convinced I've become that she knew right from the start what she was walking into. On top of that, I'm starting to believe she orchestrated that final scene with you and me."

"Orchestrated? What are you talking about?"

"Planned, designed. It was a setup."

"Are you insane? How could she have planned something like that?"

"I'm not altogether sure."

"Well if you ask me, that sounds like a big pile of psychic crap."

"Henry, there's something you don't know. Right after you finished breaking my nose."

"I broke your nose?"

"Yes. My doctor reset it."

"Shit."

"I'm fine. Just after you'd gone I opened up the metal box, and do you know what I found?"

"What?"

"A tilaka, a bindi, a third eye painted on the mirror. Now, how did that get there? I'll tell you—"

"Wait. Hold on. You're sure this thing was what you think. Not just a spot, or, I don't know, spilled ink."

"Quite sure. A perfectly symmetrical red circle."

"Wait a minute, you were bleeding like crazy. That's probably what you saw, a drop of your own blood."

"It wasn't my blood."

"Are you sure?"

"Henry, I'm telling you, I'm sure."

"If I were you I'd check, because it sounds to me like it had to have been your blood."

"Listen to me, Henry. She painted it. Understand? She painted it. I know the difference between a drop of blood and a circle of paint."

He raised his eyebrows in a disbelieving way that made me want to smack him all over again. "Okay. Fine, she painted it."

"And I'll even tell you why she did. Because she wanted to leave me a message. A message telling me she knew all along. From the day she walked in for her interview."

He snorted. "Hey, I don't want to get into another argument, but you're being incredibly self-centered. Really. I mean this is, this is way, way out there. Leaving you a message. I'm sorry, that's just not right."

"Henry, it was the third eye. 'The metaphysical point outside time and space where the absolute and the phenomenal meet.' Think about it for a second. How else did she avoid getting captured on film? There's more. Take the Old Memorial. I never told you this, but I went there to find her a second time and I made a discovery."

"You're a real detective."

"Maya checked in under the name Mara Thompson. Do you know where the name Mara comes from? No, of course not, neither did I. I looked it up. Mara is the Hindu god of lust."

"For your information, I have a cousin named Mara, and there's nothing lustful about her. Weighs over three hundred pounds. Sells junk at a flea market."

The waitress returned. "Two more?"

"Thank you." She picked up our empties. "Henry, put it in context. This Mara, not your cousin. And what about the name Old Memorial. Don't you see? Just think for a second. Jefferson, the Old Memorial. The Jefferson Memorial! A perfect fit. She must have chosen that hotel on purpose."

"Wait, wait, wait. It wouldn't be the Jefferson Memorial, it would be the Jefferson Old Memorial, or, wait, the Jefferson Old Memorial Hotel. You can't just leave words out like that. You can't pick and choose the bits to fit your version."

"Stop being so damn literal. You sound like an accountant or something. Be a little creative for once in your life. Use your mind. Interpret. It's the only explanation."

"*What* is the only explanation? You're talking as crazy as that art critic in the *Times*. Seeing what you want to see. You read some bullshit theory in a book and then the first chance you get you go out and try and turn it into real life. Really, this is funny. This is really fucking comical coming from you. The same person who once gave me such a hard time about how I supposedly misinterpreted Degas's painting. Don't you see? That's exactly what you're doing now. It's just all coincidences. Missed opportunities."

"Bad film."

"What else? You bought that film, not Maya. What else could there be? The woman's not a god. Is that what you're asking me to believe? She puts a dot on her forehead and she can suddenly turn invisible? Or are you saying she's psychic? Don't forget, you were the one who slipped up and told her you had another place nearby. Nothing psychic about that. She recognized the apartment from the paintings, just like you thought she would. You predicted it, remember? Added up the details and went home and looked around the place, or looked up at the boarded-up building across the street. She saw the reflection of the camera lens. I take full responsibility. It's my fault. I was a jerk, me. I admit it. The show was too big of an opportunity. I couldn't say no."

"Considering the *Times* article, it seems like you made the right choice."

"I don't know. Maybe I did. I was lucky, that's all. Lucky she got out of there when she did. Let's just be glad she didn't get anybody else involved. The police, Dianne Handsforth. The important thing is nobody got hurt."

"Your explanation sounds logical up to a point, but it still fails to account for the third eye on my mirror."

"Don't mess your head up with all that mystical shit. You don't even believe it yourself."

"Please refrain from telling me what I do and don't believe, Henry."

"Listen to me, it was your blood. That's the only thing it could have been."

"I refuse to accept that. I saw what I saw. Paint, Henry."

He picked up his fresh glass of champagne, downed half of it, and started scratching the back of his head.

"What?" I asked. "What are you thinking? What's the matter?"

"There's something *you* don't know."

"I'm listening."

"You know when I told you that I met her for the first time at the show?"

"Oh please. What now?"

"That wasn't technically the truth."

"Technically?"

"I, you see, I saw her a couple days before that too."

"For the love of God, Henry!"

"Now hold on. It was just for a second, when I was hanging the show. She came in for a minute, that's all."

"A second, a minute, next you're going to tell me it was an hour, two hours—"

"A minute max. I already told you what she said. Just the part about where we were from. The other day I condensed the two conversations. There isn't anything else. It was quick. She didn't say anything about the paintings. She didn't even really look at them, or I didn't think she did. I guess I was wrong—"

"Would you shut up for a second?" I yelled. The people at the surrounding tables stopped talking and stared at us. I leaned closer to him and whispered, "I can't even trust you when you're confessing. Now be clear. She first saw the paintings when, Tuesday?"

"Yes."

"Before or after I talked to you on the phone?"

"Before."

"My God. I am such a fool. Aren't I a bloody fool, Henry?"

"It didn't . . . Listen, she didn't even get a good look at them. I couldn't tell you on the phone—"

"No, of course not. By then your neck was already in the noose. That's why you made sure I wouldn't try to come to the opening. You knew she'd be there, and still you kept it from me."

"I thought—"

"Stop. I don't care what you thought. I want to hear what really happened. Start over. Tuesday. What time? What was she wearing? Be specific."

"It was around eleven in the morning. I was standing on a ladder. She walked in, alone."

"The clothes."

"Beige skirt and a white shirt. I stood there and watched her. Then she asked if Dianne was there. I came down the ladder and said she'd be in around four. I asked if she wanted me to leave a message. She said no, then asked if I was the artist. She wanted to know how long I'd been painting. It was a short conversation. We introduced ourselves and shook hands and looked at each other for a second."

"Wait. How? How did you look?"

"What? We just looked."

"I know you, Henry. You wouldn't have mentioned looking at her if there wasn't more to it. Were you flirting?"

"Jesus Christ!"

"You were, weren't you? You were working it."

"Hey, if anybody was flirting, it was her, not me."

I fought the urge to tip the table and its contents onto his lap, and leaned back in my chair, clasping my hands behind my head.

"You've got to believe me. At the time I was sure she hadn't gotten anything from the paintings. I mean, she barely looked at them. We talked all of thirty seconds and she left. I really did think it was going to all pass over and nothing would change."

"I need for you to be quiet for a minute."

"Maybe I should go."

"Stay right there."

He angled his chair for a better view of the people passing on the sidewalk and picked up his champagne flute. I stared absently at the rusting fire escape on the brick apartment building across the street and tried to meld this new information into my own story line. Ten minutes passed. I ordered us coffee.

"I'm never going to get down to the truth here, am I, Henry? There'll always be another little detail left out."

"For shit sake, there aren't more details."

"I'll never touch absolute bottom. That's the problem with getting a story secondhand, especially from someone who hasn't been especially truthful."

"What do you want me to say?"

I took a long sip of champagne. "Okay, Henry. I have no desire to insult you further. I suppose I've nobody to blame for all this but myself. I should never have trusted so much. Let's get back to how you now say it happened. You had your quick hello and asked her where she was from and where she lived, and then she left. Am I missing anything else?"

He let out a deep breath but didn't look at me. "No."

"Back to the opening. She headed straight for you and said the thing about wanting to have a word with the artist, correct?"

"Correct."

"No other revisions to report? The rest of it holding steady? Speak now. It's amnesty time."

He shook his head.

"Right. Your testimony stands." I poured cream and a sugar packet into my coffee. "Well, as far as I can tell, these new revelations don't really change much."

He hissed through his teeth.

"Listen, Henry, just because she saw the paintings earlier doesn't mean it was any less of a setup. All it means is that you're a better liar than I gave you credit for."

"All right. Let me ask you. If she did set us up, then why didn't she come bursting through the door with the police? And why hasn't she told her good friend Dianne? She sure hasn't done that. I think I'd have heard about it. Dianne's bending over backward for me. In fact, she can't wait to see more paintings. Wants another show by next year."

"A good question. What's your explanation? Why hasn't she gone to the police or Dianne?"

"You got me. The fact is she hasn't, which means it couldn't have been a setup. You don't go to all that trouble to set somebody up and then let them off the hook."

I remained quiet, but a chilling possibility ran through my mind. Perhaps Maya had been watching our fight the whole time from the other apartment. Snapping off photos as evidence. The idea was too absurd to mention, but I couldn't let go of it. Henry slid his chair back around so that he faced me and continued his line of argument.

"And say even that the spot on the mirror wasn't your blood. Fine, whatever. Think of it as a keepsake. There's your message. Big deal, she gave you something to remember her by. Hey, only a few days have passed. Did you ever think she might just be away for a while? That's still a possibility. Maybe she'll come back tomorrow. You don't know. I'd keep wearing the beard."

"Henry, even you don't believe that. How many people do you know who rent an apartment in Manhattan and then never stay there?"

"Besides you and your parents? No one."

"Drink your coffee. I'm tired of arguing with you."

"You're really serious, aren't you? You're completely spooked."

"Maybe, Henry. Maybe so."

"Jesus."

"Drink up. Let's not talk about Maya anymore."

"Fine by me." The waitress returned and I asked for the check.

•

As the days passed, a heavy malaise settled over me, and I began to wonder whether Henry wasn't right about the bindi. After all, Maya knew about my interest in the third eye from the very beginning. Maybe she did leave it for me as a simple memento, but then, what of my premonition? I didn't have the patience to try to explain it to him. Seeing what I wanted to, he'd say. No such thing as premonition. Just another instance of my paranoid mind running amok. He and I stubbornly clung to our divergent explanations, but neither of us had the means to prove them. I cursed myself for having destroyed the mirror. Could I have mistaken a drop of my own blood for the bindi? I thought about the dot so much that soon I couldn't tell if what I pictured was the actual thing or some idealized version that I shaped in my head.

Sleep came only in small doses. The circadian cycle abandoned me. My hours made no sense. I had no routine to speak of except for the stereo. There I indulged in my collection's most melancholy compositions. Notably, Shostakovich's String Quartet No. 8, which, as promised, didn't exactly cheer me up. No, this was a time to wallow.

Adrift in thought, I stopped going out and had my meals delivered. A few times I started to dial Dr. Wasserstrom's number, but I never followed through. I was too confused for therapy, I told myself. Talking to another person would only obscure matters further. My hunch that Maya had broken into my place and photographed the fight didn't pan out. I developed the roll of film inside the camera. The last shots were the ones I took of the dark, empty apartment.

Hardest of all to accept was the fact that I failed to capture her on film or canvas. Despite his newfound burst of self-confidence, I knew Henry couldn't come close to doing her from memory. He needed my photos all right. Go on then, Henry. Do your best. Hire a model or two. Archer-Handsforth was in for an unpleasant surprise. That much was sure. How long before he'd come back? I wondered. He wasn't done with his benefactor just yet.

Maya's escape remained my only real concern. An image lost to the lubricious world of memory, she'd grown that much more consuming. At once fleeting, immaterial, and ambiguous, she now embodied all the qualities I associated with a supreme work of art.

I discovered I felt no compulsion to find another girl and continue on with the experiment. No one could possibly live up to the standard Maya set. My resolve hardened with the passing days. She would be the last tenant. Despite the utter lack of encouraging signs, a part of me held out hope that I'd figure out a way to get her back. I set out for my old nemesis, the public library, without the faintest idea of what I hoped to find. Blame it on habit.

Nothing stuck in my mind on that journey. I don't recall the weather, my cabdriver, or if the streets were congested or clear. Until the moment I entered the Shoichi Noma Reading Room, the world left no aesthetic impression on me.

A single librarian occupied the room. She was a plump, middle-aged Indian woman wearing a purple and green sari. Thinking back, it sounds inconceivable, but I didn't check to see if she was wearing the bindi. I searched the shelves next to her while she stocked a stack of books. There was no sign of *Death in Banaras* nor *A Popular Dictionary of Hinduism.* I pulled out *Banaras and the Buddha* and *The Dhammapada* as well as a handful of random titles. Books on economics, politics, and wildlife. After a moment's glance at the table of contents or index, I'd trade one in for another. Slowly, all the titles blurred together, a wall of impenetrable information. After fifteen minutes I sat down empty-handed and stared off into space.

The librarian had almost finished shelving her pile of books, when she was called away by a coworker. Totally dispirited, I decided there was nothing more to do. I remember standing and turning toward the door. It was quiet. Call it chance, or fate, or God knows what, but I looked down at the only volume she hadn't yet put away. *The Book of Hindu Names* by Maneka Gandhi—a small, well-traveled, cloth-bound book. Its spine cracked and splitting, the corners of its faint red cover were frayed, and the brittle and browned pages inside felt like they were on the verge of falling away.

I glanced up at the empty room to try to dispel the strong feeling I was being watched. Each of the volumes on the shelves seemed to stare back at me. I parted the book near the middle and thumbed my way to the *M* names. There. Atop the right-hand page. Waiting for me all along. I found that clue I'd been searching out. My chest tightened and I stopped breathing. Then I read the definition aloud to my silent audience of books.

> **Maya** 1. wealth; illusion. 2. unreality; phantom; art; wisdom.

A cold, nervous tremor came over me so that I couldn't stop shaking. I snapped the book shut, stuffed it down the front of my pants, and hurried out of the room.

●

When I returned from the library, I was half out of my mind. Talking to myself in a low voice. Back again reciting every scattered detail of this story. I filled the room with words. It was a shapeless spewing that went on all night long, not even ordered enough to be called a stream of consciousness. I stared at the ceiling and talked. No eating, no music, no reading. When the phone rang I unplugged it from the wall. I didn't want anything interrupting the drone of my voice.

By dawn I could only manage a shredded whisper. I reached for a yellow notepad and tried to sketch out a time line of events, but that didn't help either. I kept adding more and more branches to the chronological trunk, and soon the page was nearly blacked out with scribbles and corrections. I decided the only way to make sure I didn't miss anything was to write it out word for word, beginning with the first day I ever heard of Maya Vanasi. The next thing I knew, I had filled fifty pages and my hand was petrified stiff from writer's cramp.

I didn't change my clothes for three days. Two notebooks finished, then three. I wrote and wrote until I came to this very chapter. Having expunged it all, I got up, put the finished product away in a desk drawer, and slept for the next twelve hours straight.

A placid dream of a long journey filled my head; it was

the kind that let me relax. I saw the ocean, then clouds passing by in a bright blue sky, foreign automobiles, different varieties of trees—spruce, birch, and Douglas fir. There was no particular structure or sequence of events. Just my mind wandering through a random series of pictures. A slide show of the subconscious.

●

Here I sit at the kitchen table of the rental apartment, writing these last few words onto a fresh yellow pad. Wednesday afternoon, just before four o'clock. An entire month has passed since my visit to the public library, a gestation period. A month without rain. A month to read, elaborate, and reflect. A month to build up my case. I spent each morning transcribing my longhand scrawl into solid type on my old Smith-Corona. Methodically, I cleared away the messy underbrush of doubt and innuendo, took a chain saw to every tree blocking my view, so that I now stare at a bald horizon. I feel transformed.

At first I didn't know whether to feel grateful to her, or bitter. Yes, I give Maya the credit. She hatched this plot for my benefit, I know that much. She tailored the setup to my idiosyncrasies from the very beginning. One by one I examined the sticking points, and I'm more certain than ever she planned the whole thing far ahead of time. Lining up and inspecting them in their aggregate, it's easy to see the premeditation of her conspiracy. It reminds me of the way I warned Henry that the cumulative gist in the details of the Victoria series would give us away. Alone, any one might not be cause for alarm. Assembled together, they are a magnifying glass.

I began uncovering her plot when I reread her reaction to

our tour of the apartment. Most important, her fascination with Degas's "Interior." The way she stood gazing at it made me believe it had an emotional effect on her, but I'm now inclined to think it was all an act. Yes. She stopped there because she knew the painting signified the link to Henry. Because the reproduction marked the moment Henry broke through and accepted the role of the voyeur. Whether or not she consciously knew as much—and I believe she did—doesn't really matter. The fact remains, she instantaneously sensed the painting's importance. She was a dowsing branch curling toward a hidden well.

The same holds true for the bathtub. I wrongly implied she never used it. During our interview I reduced her curiosity to a simple love for bathing, but again I missed the larger significance. Take her own words. "I'm partial to measurements." More metaphors, of course. The measuring itself was a calculated, symbolic action meant to show me she knew what I was doing—evaluating and deceiving her. Why else go to the trouble of getting down on her hands and knees?

Next, the Old Memorial and the name Mara. I maintain she brought me to that hotel on purpose, and furthermore, that the reason she called me Mr. Jefferson was not due to any supposed misunderstanding. She discerned I'd borrowed it from the Founding Father, and in return started playing her own name games, leading me to the hotel and its dilapidated red-and-white sign swinging above the door. The damaged portion had faded in such a way that viewing it from a half-block away, as I did the other morning on a reconfirming cab ride, the words appeared to read:

The

Memorial
Hotel

That space between "The" and "Memorial" practically cried out for the insertion of "Jefferson," hence the Jefferson Memorial— sorry, Henry. And the word "hotel"? Well, wasn't I running a kind of hotel each summer?

Such a subtle and playful spirit she was. What is a memorial anyway? A place to remember the dead. If I were a quicker wit, maybe I'd have caught on sooner. By leading me to the hotel, she foretold Jefferson's demise. Jefferson the alter ego, I mean.

Inside, I discovered even more trickery. Mara, the Temptress. That name and a corroborating definition sit on the page before "Maya" in *The Book of Hindu Names*. The god of lust and sin. Certainly, my own lust brought me to Harlem. She planted the deity on the page for me, knowing there was just enough inconsistency to keep me from nailing her down. The switch from Maya to Mara seemed close enough, but Vanasi to Thompson? One of the Western world's most common names, Thompson was a brilliant touch of realism meant to give me pause, as was her writing London as her home city. If she'd said Manchester, I wouldn't have hesitated in definitively linking the two of them. Meticulously, she assembled a scenario just imperfect enough so as to probe the limits of my greed for a coherent explanation.

Next came the disconcerting discovery of Mara's check-in date: Friday, June 25, the day after Maya's interview. For a long time this confounded me. I thought it might be a detail I'd never reconcile into my theory, as it seemed convincing proof that Mara and Maya were two different people. Then, on the third or fourth time through the yellow notepads, I saw something I'd missed—the out-of-date calendar on the lobby wall. June 1989. After many late-night hours pacing the length of my apartment, the obvious popped into my thick head. On the twenty-fifth of June, back in 1989, I interviewed Laura and officially began the sublet portion of my experiment. I remember the exact date because I circled it on a checkbook calendar. I went to my file cabinet and dug out the old ledger just to make sure.

When I examined it and the circle of red ink around the number 25, my mind flew into a series of fragile calculations. How had Maya figured out the significance of the date? Could she have surveilled me all these years? I thought back to the eerie passage from *Death in Banaras,* "It [Banaras] stands outside of space and time and yet all space is contained within it. . . ." And once more to the definition of the bindi: "The metaphysical point out of time and space . . ." Perhaps the third eye allowed her to see through layers of time. I confess I was in over my head, and I could hear Henry's heavy, condescending voice upon my shoulder telling me to calm down.

Eventually, I gave up my layman attempts to solve the space-time riddle, but what came clear in it all was that the threshold separating coincidence from conscious act had been broken. The expired calendar and the repetition of June 25 were not random occurrences. She used them as props, just as she used the name Mara. Whether or not the decrepit staff at the Old Memorial aided her in this regard remains unclear. Maya could have put up a different calendar every hour for a week and I don't think they would have noticed. And as for the absence of her name in the hotel book? I can't say for sure, but I refer to my own description of the registration log itself. "It looked like they'd used it for years, erasing and reentering names as their guests came and went." Maybe Maya simply erased her name and added Mara's two days later.

I moved on in search of other loose threads and landed on Dianne Handsforth. Could Henry really believe that if the two women were good friends, Maya wouldn't have told Dianne about our scheme? Or perhaps he'd deluded himself into thinking his new gallery pimp was protecting him from the law, turning a blind eye because she wanted to protect her investment. The truth is Maya never told Dianne Handsforth about the apartment. In fact, I'm willing to bet they never actually met. I came upon this especially humbling finding a few evenings back as I was reclining on the living room couch with Gustav Mahler and a bottle of single malt scotch. I got up, retrieved the freshly typed pages from the kitchen table, and went over Henry's testimony regarding the show and the hanging of it.

No, he'd never seen the two of them together. If one can believe his final version—and one doesn't have much of a choice—Maya walked into the gallery claiming to be looking for Dianne but didn't bother to leave a message. Furthermore, at the opening the two women did not interact. Dianne approached with someone for Henry to meet and Maya disappeared. Why wouldn't Dianne also introduce the man to Maya?

I called Henry right then and asked whether or not Maya attended the dinner afterward. "Jesus!" he said with a sigh. "Why don't you drop it already? I'm starting to get seriously worried about you. You sound like you're losing it."

"Yes or no, Henry. That's all I need."

"No."

"You're sure?"

"Absolutely, one hundred percent. No, she wasn't there."

I hung up and went outside to a pay phone around the corner. "Sag Harbor, Long Island please. A residence . . ."

I inserted more coins and dialed. A female housekeeper answered. "Handsforth residence. Good day."

"Yes, hello. I'm trying to reach a houseguest. Maya Vanasi."

"No, I'm sorry, sir. No one here by that name," she said in an officious tone.

"You're sure of it? Perhaps a few weeks ago she stayed there."

"Who is this please?"

I put the receiver down and started to laugh. So perfectly played, Maya. Well done. She guessed right that the fear of being caught would keep Henry from asking Dianne about her. Such gullibility on both our parts. The odds of a tourist in a city of twelve million befriending the gallery owner of Henry's next show. That same tourist landing the sublet. Hindsight, how perfect you are!

"What's in a name?" she said during our lunch at Fleur de Lis. Quite a lot, it turns out. Which definition best describes her? I wonder. Wealth, illusion, unreality, phantom, art, or wisdom? Each one so ripe in the context of the story. But why limit myself to a single reading? After all, the viability of multiple interpretations appears to have been a running theme in this mess. The disputed title of "Interior," for instance, all the words and meanings for the dot on her forehead, not to mention the unnameable variety of my agoraphobia. What is in a name, Maya?

The fact I'm even arguing the use of a theme and metaphor—qualities reserved for works of art—proves the setup theory all the more. Metaphor and theme aren't found in true realism, they're mental constructs. And construct them she did in this grand and personalized work of art.

Far from a merely decorative piece, Maya's conceptual masterpiece served a functional purpose. She came down—from what place or heaven I do not know—to tell me it was time to move on, to put an end to the experiment, the agoraphobia, and the partnership with Henry. I'd exhausted all the artistic possibilities of voyeurism but couldn't break away from the routine. I thank her for showing me that, for it was just a matter of time before we got caught and put in jail.

Even if Henry never paints a decent picture again, I see now that the split with him was for the best. As for me, I'll begin fresh with some other project. New themes to explore, new methods to try. Poor Henry. He may have a rough few years when he finds his keen eye for detail has left him. Maybe he'll adapt and find another mechanism, or maybe his fifteen minutes have passed. He dropped by yesterday morning with a bag of espresso and the newspaper from my doorstep. I cleared the typewriter and the stack of papers from the kitchen table and put some water on. "So," he said in a doctor's tone. "How are you feeling?"

"Must you sound as though I've just escaped from a mental ward? Sit down."

"Sorry. I see you're still typing away at that thing."

"Almost finished."

"It's practically a novel. How many pages is it?"

"Many."

"I guess if it helps you."

"Don't suppose you'd be interested in reading it."

He leaned back so that his chair balanced on its hind legs. "You still think it was a trap from some spirit above?"

"You can stop with that voice, Henry. In fact, forgive me, but the truth is I'm not in a very social mood. I'd like to be left alone to write. I'm close to finishing."

"Should I come by in a few days?"

"If you like. Thanks for the coffee." He got up and gave me one last excruciatingly heartfelt look of concern before leaving.

Believe what you must, Henry. I know I do. There's no point in his reading this. Even if I did show him these pages, he'd shrug them off as a bad interpretation. He said "novel," of course, meaning a fictional work. I guess I can't blame him. He didn't live through it the way I did. Thomas Hardy had it right.

"A senseless school where we must give our lives that we may learn to live."

It's no use trying to change another person's mind after it's made up, especially concerning matters of faith. I've no choice but to embrace that shadowy expanse. How my father will bristle. Though it may be true, as he claims, that faith is nothing but the inability to scientifically prove a point of view, these days that doesn't sound so awful. If I've learned one thing from Maya, it's that even the most rational mind can't answer every question. I'll never know, for instance, the how of it all. How she pulled it off, or how the third eye functions. I suppose it's absurd to think someone in the phenomenal realm could hope to understand the workings of the absolute—bindi or no bindi.

I placed my ad in this week's paper, and I've been sitting by the phone the whole night through. I let the answering machine pick up and I screen each call for the voice I hardly remember. Her voice. No, the apartment isn't available to just anybody. This isn't a cattle call, nor is it an act of desperation. I decided to give it one last stab simply to put a palindromic ending on it. Later this evening, when it's finally finished, I'll head back home and punch out the last weary letters on the typewriter.

This morning I confirmed my plane reservation to the South of France. My parents don't know yet. I'd like to surprise them. Catch my father covered in chocolate, wearing a floppy French chef's hat. Mother by the pool of some hotel, lying in a chaise longue, her back glistening with sun oil. Yes, Mother, you heard right. I'm leaving this island. It's time to put this agoraphobia business behind me.

Three days ago I conducted the first test. I removed the baffles from the apartment windows and looked out at the long view down Sullivan Street without incident. Morning sunlight streamed in and lit up the darkroom. Across the way the fifth floor lay deathly still, a fact that no longer bothered me. At last I'm free to leave my home without worrying what I might miss. Now that the experiment is done with, my hope is the illness, too, has passed. I'll see what rural France has to say about it.

The calls come in a steady stream. After each one I press the erase button and reset. In my lap I hold *The Book of Hindu Names*. I carry it with me wherever I go, bookmarked to the same page. Beside me stands a large bottle of Evian, a blank application, a Polaroid camera, a new package of film, and a bowl containing a single foil-wrapped piece of carob. Chopin's waltzes glide out of the stereo. An order of freshly delivered sushi waits on the table in front of me, but I've barely touched it, nor have I opened the bottle of Riesling. After she left, my powerful food cravings receded, and I've taken to substituting appetizer portions for my main course. "Moderate in my food," *The Dhammapada* would say.

All I want now, all I humbly ask, is the opportunity for another meeting. So I cast out this metaphysical bait, prepared for what may or may not come. I offer it up with the full concession of defeat. Maya has won. She succeeded in framing me more succinctly than I could have ever captured her. I'm sure she's watching even now. No doubt with a smile upon her lips.

If she does come, I won't insist on taking her picture. To lay my eyes on that work of art again would more than suffice. No words or questions will be necessary. I'll just sit quietly with my legs crossed, a thoughtful hand on my chin, and admire her. Of course, I don't expect she'll grant this request. Indeed, after taking me this far, why ruin a moment of aesthetic perfection?